DRIFTING

BY KATIA D. ULYSSE

Published by Akashic Books
©2014 Katia D. Ulysse

Cover art: *Aftermath* by Jean-Robert Simeon (acrylic on canvas, 2010), courtesy of Katia D. Ulysse.

ISBN-13: 978-1-61775-240-7
Library of Congress Control Number: 2013956776

Akashic Books
Twitter: @AkashicBooks
Facebook: AkashicBooks
E-mail: info@akashicbooks.com
Website: www.akashicbooks.com

for Felicie Montfleury, James M.,
Juliêtte M. Jave, and Jeanika Ulysse

TABLE OF CONTENTS

PART I

THE LEAST OF THESE

THE LEAST OF THESE

There was a time when you could drop a fishbone in Puits Blain's soil and it would grow into a whale. During those days, wealthy gran nègs nicknamed Puits Blain "Sweet Place." It was far enough away from their mansions in Pétionville, but close enough for a Saturday-morning jaunt to some great-aunt's mud-and-thatched-roof hut. How serene it all was back then! Even snakes knew to keep their eggs in the old cast-iron pots in the calabash grove. No one knew how those pots got under the calabash trees; it had been generations since anyone even cared to ask. Some said ancestors used those pots to cook the medicine that clamped slave women's wombs shut. No matter. Manman always scolded my sister and me whenever she caught us playing near those pots. As soon as she would look away, we'd go right back to our games.

Manman went the way of the ancestors years ago. She died of a broken heart on account of the fact that Papa sold her land right out from underneath her, and went on to scatter his own seed from Port-au-Prince to Port-de-Paix.

Freda and I came to the United States to study. My sister had such a way with books that she earned a top spot at the John Hopkins School of Medicine. I, on the other hand, had only songs in my brain. Morning, noon, and night, all I wanted to do was write songs. Most days I woke up with one in my head—intro, bridge, and all—like a Christmas gift that had not been there the previous night.

Freda and her medical degree returned to Puits Blain when Hurricane Jeanne orphaned more children than anyone could count. Her house/clinic was not far from where we grew up. The mud huts had been replaced by concrete-block dwellings. As for the calabash groves, someone sold those gourd, limb, and root. The old cast-iron pots were gone too. Sweet Place had become a maze of alleyways; few people made it out, not to work or interact with outsiders. Each house—with its crown of twisted rebar—received an additional bedroom (or a second floor) as soon as a dollar dropped by. The dream was always to add one more room; one more story on the rooftop, until the house came close to resembling a gran nèg's mansion. Not much sweetness left in Puits Blain now; just layers upon layers of dust.

Sometimes Freda's orphaned children seemed to die just from the dust. I'd been tempted once or twice to bring one home with me, especially since nine doctors in as many states swore my womb was defective. Of course, there were umpteen medical procedures available to women like myself. I tried them all. Nothing took. After years of "trying," Serge (my husband) and I withdrew our petition from Nature's court, and traded our baby-making budget for an extended vacation.

Our luxurious suite had a private pool so wide it merged with the sky and the sea. Serge and I took advantage of the heavenly views and treated ourselves to good old-fashioned sex morning, noon, and night. For the first time in ages we didn't treat our bodies like vending machines that stole our money but kept our goodies trapped behind some faulty metal spiral.

It was not until two months after we returned from our vacation that I noticed menses had stopped making an appearance. One particular suspicion nibbled at my heart, but I didn't dare give in to it until the Extra-Thyme Soap and Body Potion woman looked at me and gushed: *Michelle, girl, I know that glow!*

I purchased a home pregnancy test; read and reread the directions a few times before using it. When I saw the Extra-Thyme woman again, I gave her permission to add *psychic* to her list of gifts.

I called my gynecologist for an appointment. My life was about to change. I needed confirmation.

"Congratulations!" the doctor intoned. Wide, scrutinizing eyes were partly condemnatory, partly approving. Hadn't she told me this would never happen?

"Can you believe it?" I asked her.

She assured me that in her line of work there wasn't much she had not seen. So, yes, she could believe it.

I thought about tricking Serge into joining me at his favorite restaurant and slipping a note into his pumpkin pie, but we'd been through too much for that. I called his cell phone and said: "We're pregnant, chéri."

"We're going to have a boy!" Serge shouted.

Next, I telephoned my sister. Freda congratulated me as if I'd won a championship with one second left on the clock. "If you need me," she said, "I'll be on the next plane." I would never ask Freda to leave her work. That clinic was all the children had for miles.

* * *

I spent the first trimester memorizing *What to Expect When You're Expecting*. Serge and I declined the "highly recommended—particularly in your case" amniocentesis. The doctor took every opportunity to remind us that my pregnancy was "high risk," due in part to my advanced age of thirty-six. We would keep our baby whatever the prognosis, we knew this. Also, we decided that boy or girl, we would name our child Dieudonne. Serge was not particularly religious, but there was no question this baby was a gift from God. A few months later, during one of our endless sonograms, the doctor confirmed our baby was a boy; Serge nearly collapsed with joy.

One morning when Dieudonne tried to karate-chop his way out without any assistance from me or a doctor, Serge rushed me to the emergency room. A team of doctors poked, prodded, and photographed me inside and out. Serge and I kept our eyes on the monitor, watching our little Dieudonne's fully developed face. The pursed lips said he would have his own opinions and voice them whenever and however he chose. Little fists were ready for battle. The umbilical cord appeared to be wound around his neck. He seemed to be resting from all the thrashing around he had done earlier.

"How is the baby?" Serge and I asked the doctor.

The doctor's posture slackened when she informed us in an apologetic tone how there appeared to be "umbilical complications."

Our baby was born that morning. The doctor asked what name we had chosen. Serge squeezed my hand and said we didn't have to use *that* name.

"No hurry," the doctor said, not looking at Serge or me now that she had been shoved from her upper rung of authority. "This is a difficult time," she added superfluously.

"Dieudonne," I told her through clenched teeth. "My son's name is Dieudonne."

Serge and I held each other and cried for a long time. When we returned to our house, we drifted like deflated balloons between rooms. Years ago, when we converted our garage to a recording studio, Serge had joked the commute was hard on his feet. Perhaps that was why he lived there now. Music, his loyal concubine, kept him busy all the time. I stayed in our bedroom.

When I called Freda to tell her what had happened, she said, "Take heart, you'll get pregnant again." I thanked her, knowing there would not be a next time.

Several months after Dieudonne, Serge and I tried but still couldn't get on with the business of being. The fact was, we mourned best alone—one of those details couples don't discover about themselves until they're submerged in a crisis. We kept to our own spaces, sparing our marriage the strain. Nothing would have been worse than to follow "umbilical complications" with a divorce.

I used to love to work with Serge in his studio. He would give me a microphone and I would make up a melody to go with whatever he was playing. Now, I stayed in the bedroom. Neither music nor Serge interested me.

My husband had a reputation for mixing down songs in such a way that would reach into your very soul. For that reason, Protestant groups brought him music project after project. They came with tambourines, violins, and choirs of men and women with clashing but angelic voices. January was always a busy month for Serge. The Protestants wanted their CDs in time for Easter; konpa bands had to have their theme song ready for Kanaval. "It's going to be awhile before I can touch your stuff," Serge would tell the Protestants. The upcoming Kanaval in Port-au-Prince took precedence. Even God knew that.

Serge was standing in the bedroom. His eyes had a faraway look in them. "How's it going?" he asked reluctantly, knowing what my answer would be.

I said nothing.

The snowflakes in his hair glistened like crushed glass. He stared at the floor, not sure how to proceed. He would return to the studio in a few seconds. I would not see him again for hours, maybe the next day.

"What are you working on?" I asked.

"Kanaval stuff." He almost smiled. The New Year was ten days old already; the rapture that was Kanaval was fast approaching.

"When are you leaving?" I managed a smile.

"I don't plan to go this year," Serge said, turning to leave.

I sat up for a better look at the imposter pretending to be my husband. This would be the first time Serge would miss Kanaval in all the years since we'd known each other. "You *will* go," I announced. "And I'm going with you."

When I was five years old, a chaloska clown on stilts

startled me so much that I tumbled down a ravine, breaking my legs. Another time, a man covered in tar had spread his makeshift wings so wide and shouted words so terrifying through grotesque strap-on lips that I hid in one of the old cast-iron pots in the calabash grove. There I was now, telling my husband how lovely it would be to revisit the mayhem of Kanaval.

"There's always next year," Serge said, shoulders sagging.

"We're going *this* year." I jumped out of bed and parted the curtains, letting in the winter light. The street was fluorescent with snow. I opened the windows, letting the stale air out. Serge watched with a frightened look in his eyes.

"My husband will not miss Kanaval in 2010 or any other year." I pumped my fist like a martyr at the gallows. The wintry air began to congeal the pockets of grief inside me. The sights and sounds of Kanaval would help Serge and me forget our troubles, if only for a while. Being in Haiti might even jolt us into being a couple again.

"I'll think about it," he whispered, then walked out of the bedroom backward, half-expecting me to foam at the mouth or something. I pulled the bedsheets off. The mattress needed to breathe.

I purchased two nonrefundable airline tickets online, then called Freda to tell her that Serge and I would arrive in two days.

"Bring your dancing shoes," Freda said with one of those cautious laughs people reserve for the bereaved.

I took a much-needed bath and put a dab of Coco

Chanel behind each ear. When I joined Serge in the studio, he put his arms around me. "You smell good," he said.

My stomach growled when I noticed the scattered remains of Chinese food on a table. I hadn't eaten anything that day, nor had I eaten dinner the night before. Serge read my mind and said he would order sandwiches from a nearby deli.

We attacked our food the moment it arrived. When we finished, Serge played with the knobs on his sprawling sound board, transforming the studio into a digital version of the earthen-floor vodun temple where he grew up drumming at ceremonies.

"I think I have a new song," I told him.

Serge gave me a full smile for the first time in an eternity.

It was a blustery dawn when we began our four-hour plane ride to Port-au-Prince. The plane burst with college-aged sets in matching *Pray for Haiti Now!* and *Save Haiti Today!* T-shirts. They boasted about their plans for saving the so-called poorest nation in the Western hemisphere. They congratulated one another on their novel ideas. They would do what Haitians could not do for themselves. They would Tweet and post proof of their hard work on social networking sites. I put my head on Serge's shoulder and forced myself to sleep.

When we reached Freda's place it was not yet noon. "It takes more time to get to LA from our house," Serge quipped. "We should come to Haiti at least once a week." His eyes sparkled. The subtle film of perspiration on his face made him glow.

Freda had bought a lavish meal of fried plantains, fish, and rice for us. Serge and I ate as if we had not seen food in months. Freda, of course, could not join us at the table. There were two children in her care. She dared not leave them.

"You're a saint," Serge told Freda.

"Anybody could do what I do," Freda replied, bowing her head. The utilitarian dress hanging from her thin frame betrayed no curves. Her hair was cropped like a soldier's. "Go enjoy the Caribbean sun," she instructed us. She would not leave the children for a moment. They were, after all, the ones she had meant to have *someday*— if only there had been time.

Serge and I went outside to sit on the washerwoman's heap of rocks. All around us, concrete-block dwellings were stacked like dominoes with dots for windows and dots for doors. The calabash groves were but a memory.

"Honè," said a woman trudging up to Freda's place with a child in her arms. Sweat dripped off the face of a boy inching behind her.

Serge and I rose from our pile of rocks to greet them.

"Doktè a la?" the woman asked in one quick breath. The child in her arms coughed violently; the rusty eyes offered an apology.

"The doctor is here," I replied in Creole, and called Freda.

With outstretched arms, Freda rushed to greet her visitors. "Bonjou," she spoke quickly. She needed to return to the children inside the clinic.

"My baby caught the illness," the woman declared. Tears pooled in her eyes. "This illness put my husband under the ground last month." The child in her arms convulsed, as if to underscore the woman's words.

"Give her to me," Freda said, taking the baby. The woman followed Freda into the clinic.

"I'm going with them," I told Serge, and followed the women.

"What's her name?" Freda asked, as she placed the child in a worn crib.

"Dieudonne," the woman said.

Something inside me leapt.

"And you, madame? What is your name?" Freda asked.

"Lidia."

What did names matter at this time?

Freda wiped her brow. "Hot day, yes?"

"Yes," Lidia replied, eyes narrowing. "This is Haiti. All the days are hot."

Freda would not tell Lidia that she did not like to be rushed. She would do everything she could to save Dieudonne's barely used life. "Dieudonne means *God gives*," Freda added.

"Is that so?" Lidia and I chorused in unison.

Freda listened with her stethoscope to the story that Dieudonne's lungs were dying to tell.

"Go play outside," Lidia said to the lanky boy clinging to her skirt. "Wait for me there."

"I stay with you," the boy bleated.

"Do it." Lidia wagged her finger.

The boy did not budge. I took his hands, and said: "Come with me."

"Take him to your lounge chair under the sun," Freda

suggested with a forced smile. "This is your island get-away, remember?"

I led the boy to the washerwoman's heap of rocks. Serge was now talking to a passerby a few feet away. The boy and I sat in silence for a time. When I asked his name, he said: "Everyone calls me Ti Papa. I don't like it, but I accept it." His were bold, unblinking eyes.

"Why do they call you that?"

"I look like my father, but I don't want to die like him."

"You won't die," I said.

Ti Papa shrugged, then asked: "Why didn't *you* want to stay inside?"

"I'm not a doctor."

"You have a soft heart," Ti Papa said. "You can't have a soft heart if you're here to save lives. Sometimes you have to break a bone to save the rest of the body. You cannot have a soft heart if you have to break bones." The boy's eyes stayed fixed on the domino dwellings in the distance, searching for some unknown thing. He was a wise old man trapped in a child's body.

"The doctor made me leave," Lidia explained contritely when she joined us on the rocks moments later. "It won't help Dieudonne to see me sad."

Ti Papa once again became withdrawn, childlike, and clung to his mother's skirt.

"If anyone can take care of Dieudonne, it's Freda," I told Lidia, hoping this was not another wish that would not come true.

"So they say," Lidia replied. "Children deserve a better life." She gestured at the concrete dwellings around us and sighed heavily. "I want to give my children a decent life, but I don't see how. A good future is not possible in this country. I would give my two arms to find a better way."

As Lidia opened her mouth to speak again, the washerwoman's heap of rocks shook so forcefully we jumped to our feet and stared at the ground in disbelief. Shock registered in Ti Papa's eyes as the rocks bounced on the arid soil and rolled around like marbles. Lidia peered about for a clue of what was happening. The ground under our feet looked like a stormy sky. It grumbled like thunder, and cracked like lightning. Water gushed out from sudden fissures in the desertlike soil. Earth and sky had been inverted, and Paradise was lost. The angry earth lifted and then dropped us with a vengeance. A piercing scream ripped through Lidia's throat as she reached for Ti Papa, but something under the ground pushed the boy even further away. Serge ran toward me, screaming something but I could not hear because the domino houses were now crumbling like stale cake, one on top of the other on top of the other, sending explosions of dust skyward.

All around us, the dwellings continued to fall. There was thick dust in my eyes, dust in my mouth. There was a dust storm in the spot where Freda's clinic had been only moments before.

I screamed for my sister. Lidia screamed for Dieudonne. I realized then that I had never learned the other two children's names. Ti Papa held his mother's skirt and shook violently. The parched terrain underneath us shook even more violently.

"Dear God," Serge shrieked as he made his way to the mound of concrete blocks that had been Freda's clinic. "Dear God," he repeated as he began to remove cement blocks and toss them aside. He would not stop until he rescued Freda and the babies she had meant to have—if only there'd been time.

BEREAVEMENT PAY

Come on in, dear. Sit down. Would you like some coffee? Hey, how often does the boss ask if you'd like something to drink? Times are changing, aren't they? Some say the world is coming to an end. I hope they're wrong. By the way, has everyone in your family been accounted for? Never mind that question. You must be getting sick of hearing it. People must ask you that all the time. Has everyone in your family been accounted for? That is an odd question. After all, it's been weeks since the quake struck. I hope you don't hold it against me for asking you this now. I've been busy with life. You know how it is.

I hear communication is still pretty bad between here and there; hear it's tough getting through. Have you been able to reach your people? From what I understand communication was pretty below standard even before this thing happened. I'm guessing you don't know much of anything. Who would? Come to think of it, you may never know if all your family is accounted for. Dear God!

Listen, dear, I understand. I really do. I've even had a nightmare or two. If I were in your shoes, I don't know what I would do. I can't even begin to wrap my brain around some of the images I've seen on CNN. I can't imagine what your people must be going through. The scope of this mess is like nothing the world has ever seen. Dead bodies in wheelbarrows. Dead bodies being shoveled into mass graves. Blood everywhere. Dust and blood. No one has a name. No one is accounted for, right?

This sort of thing must never happen on US soil. I've got kids, you know: a boy and a girl, plus one on the way. Can you imagine? I don't know what I would do if something like that happened here.

Even our military guys down in your country are having a difficult time. And some of those guys have done tours in Iraq, Afghanistan. They say your country has the desert beat by a thousand miles. I read somewhere that the soldiers now have trouble sleeping. They can't keep food down. They're going to need serious assistance after this quake thing blows over. War, you know, is different. You expect to see certain things on the battlefield. You expect to hear certain noises, cries. You expect to smell certain smells. You expect to see death. A lot of it, in fact. But this is not war.

My heart goes out to you, dear. And to your family. Believe me when I tell you that. My heart goes out to your country too. I'd never heard so much about that place in my entire life before the quake hit.

You know, I became so interested and curious that I started to do a little research myself. I had no idea you guys were the first black republic. 1804, right? That's pretty impressive. I saw something about the maroon people: slaves so clever no one could catch them. It was cool the way they hid in those hills. I'll have to go back and read a little more about them. I like to know about that sort of thing.

I found out your country used to be gorgeous too. Imagine that! It was the place to be once upon a time, am I right? They called it the Pearl, or something like that. That sounds so resort-like, you know: *Come on down to the Pearl. Lose your shoes and your troubles. Have a cocktail with one of those little umbrellas in them.* Somebody told me Elizabeth Taylor and other movie stars used to vacation down there. I hear Bill and Hillary Clinton honeymooned down there. Who knew Haiti was a place to have a honeymoon?

Hey, can you believe your country is next to the Dominican Republic? It's like one of those masks you see in the theater: comedy and tragedy, right? I've taken my family to the DR several times. Nice place. Amazing beaches. Good food! You'd never know your country was right next door.

Yes . . . of course . . . forgive me . . . Here I am going on and on, telling you what you probably already know. Believe me when I tell you I really, truly do feel your pain. I can almost put myself in your shoes. So, let's get back to your question about bereavement pay.

Yes. If you consult the employee manual, you'll see how bereavement is broken down according to proximity. Your mind might be all jumbled up right now with all that you must be going through. Mine would be too. So let me help you find the information you need:

If you lose a mother or a father, that's an automatic five days off. With pay. If you lose a sister or a brother, three days, also with pay. Grandparents: two days (but you only get paid for one). First cousins: one day, without pay. An uncle or an aunt—depending on how close you were to them, half a day (and we'll need proof, of course . . . you know . . . something to show you were actually at a memorial service . . . you understand . . . oh . . . wait . . . in your case . . . given the circumstances . . . well, how do I put this? . . . given what we've all seen on TV . . . you won't be required to provide that sort of proof).

Back to the list. Yes . . . second cousins. Let's see. No . . . they're not on the list. You would not be allowed time off per se, but there's always your lunch hour. At any rate, you can see, second cousins are not on the list. Your mother-in-law's brother on her father's side . . . no, also not on the list . . . Your cousin's sister on his mother's side . . . nope, sorry . . . The lady who took care of you for ten years while your parents immigrated to another country to work and send money so you could eat and go to school . . . sorry, not on the list either . . . The lady's children? Come on, are you kidding me?

PART II

FLORA

THE HUNTERS

Her black curls glistened in the sunlight streaming through a hole in the corrugated tin roof. Take away those layers of dust and the spider webs crisscrossed on her lace-trimmed bib; take away that three-inch long crack in her right leg; anyone would have mistaken her for a real baby—a good, well-behaved baby, waiting patiently for her bottle of warm milk with a spoonful of powdered rice thrown in.

Nine years later and I still wonder what happened to that doll. She did not fall out of the high chair and drag her fractured limb out of the house. I searched everywhere for days. For years I entertained the fantasy that a street child had crept upstairs and taken the doll. But no one had broken into our house. The landlord must have lied. Nothing mysterious about that. Grown-ups lied all the time, to one another and to kids. Especially to kids: *Be a good girl, sweetie, and take this balloon to the latrine for me. Don't untie the knot. Don't try to blow it up either. It's a special kind of balloon. It's no good once it's been used. And it's been used. Heh! Heh!*

Of course the landlord lied. I can still hear him talking to Manman as if she were a child: "See that door at the top of the stairs? Don't ever open it. You won't pay rent for the room behind it. So pretend it's not there

. . . Oh, you see a doll through the keyhole? Just ignore it. My last tenant had kids too. Three girls, like you. The doll must have belonged to them. Look, madame, if you don't want to rent the house, hurry up and say so. I've got fifteen other people lined up."

"Mister, please." Manman had been nervous. She needed that house for two reasons: the rent was the cheapest she had found anywhere, and the school which my sisters and I would attend was so close we could see our classrooms from the front porch.

Manman dared not look into the landlord's eyes. "How many months do you want in advance, mister?"

"Two will do." The man kept his own eyes on the sweetsop tree behind Manman.

"Two?" Usually, landlords were not so kind. Manman had expected him to ask for at least four months in advance.

"Yes, two."

"God bless you." Manman thumbed through the spectrum of Haitian currency in her hands: blue, brown, orange. A couple of green US dollars sat on the stack like icing on a cake.

The landlord took the money from Manman and counted it. When he was done, he said: "Welcome to your new home, madame." A friendly smile played on his lips. He knew all along that Manman would take the house.

"Thank you, mister. Bon Dye va beni w. God will bless you."

The landlord had his reasons for keeping us out of the doll room. Nine years later and I still wonder what those reasons were. Flora Desormeau, I tell myself, forget the doll. But I can't forget—just as I cannot forget the day Manman came home late and as a routine peeped through that keyhole. "Where is she?" Manman was so distraught that the doll was gone she said it was time for us to leave the house too. She fished out her dog-eared Bible and the long list of highly recommended psalms that she carried in her purse for protection—like a switchblade or a loaded gun. She gestured for me to start reading while she crossed herself hurriedly.

"*Dans ma détresse, c'est à l'Éternel que je crie*," I began. "*In my distress I cried unto the Lord . . .*"

Of all the chores I was expected to do in our house, reading the psalms with Manman was the most tedious. She repeated each word in that exaggerated lilt of the illiterate. Her stubborn tongue refused to contort itself around the French vowels. Her mouth had never been trained to make those strange sounds. She parted her lips when puckering and stretching them was necessary. The pointed "u" came out like "ee." The unnatural "e" sounded like the English "a."

I was tired and justifiably unnerved about the missing doll myself. Manman, on the other hand, was alert, vigilant. Each time I skipped a line or two to try and make the reading go faster, she made me start from the beginning. She had memorized the Bible in its entirety—or so it seemed—and was now reciting the psalms verbatim. She was not simply echoing me. She paused for the punctuation marks, even before I saw them: one second for commas, two for periods. She stopped between verses like a child looking both ways before crossing the street. Manman did not need me.

"Do we have to read all of these tonight?" I protested.

Manman did not appreciate the question nor did she care for my tone of voice. Her hand shot up to slap me. Since we were praying, she decided against it. I continued to read while Manman followed along from her impeccable memory: "*Lève-toi, Éternel! Sauve-moi . . . Tu brises les dents des méchants . . . Arise, O Lord! Save me . . . You break the teeth of the wicked . . .*"

"This will take hours," I said.

"Quit whining!" Manman shouted in Creole.

The kerosene lamp on the floor next to me filled my throat with so much smoke that it itched. My mouth was dry.

"Keep reading."

I read until a rooster crowed and the sun rolled out of bed and the streets buzzed with the protests of children fetching water from distant streams.

"Amen," I said after the last word of the last psalm on Manman's endless list.

"Amen." Manman sounded like she'd been haggling with a vendor at the marketplace over a can of tomato paste. She closed the Bible, keeping her eyes on the worn leather. She did not blink. It was the book's turn to agree to or counter whatever secret offer she'd made. After a few minutes of silent bargaining, she put the Bible away, saying, "If that doesn't do it, nothing will."

While the streets filled with vendors, their wares in large baskets on their heads, the sun and the moon engaged in a hostile battle: one defied the other to try and rise before or linger beyond its allotted time. The few stars that lagged behind to watch the scuffle gave up their good seats, taking their light elsewhere. The outcome was too predictable: the sun would prevail. It always did in Haiti. From the moment it rose each morning until it went down, it spread its scorching power over everything that stood between the mountains and the sea, raging like a sugarcane field set on fire at harvest time.

Manman sectioned my hair into three parts and braided them. Two of the braids stopped just above my ears. The third, at the top of my head, stuck up in the air like a tiny stump in freshly raked black soil. Manman then ordered me to wear my green dress for good luck, in case the psalms failed. She wore a coat-dress with large buttons that ran from her neck to her ankles. It had been sent to her by someone in the States who forgot the definition of tropical. Our roses did not wither in December. Bougainvillea blossoms did not succumb to wintry nights. Hibiscus blooms did not steal away to some subterranean retreat—like peonies and irises had a habit of doing in the States. Our flowers did not hibernate in unmarked graves for seasons at a time. They showed themselves unabashedly, January through December, never losing their vibrancy. The breadfruit, the mango, the avocado, the palm—none of our trees found it necessary to expel every last one of their leaves in autumn. Temperatures never dipped to freezing. No one expected snow to fall on Christmas Day or New Year's Eve. Women did not need to cover themselves with dresses such as the one Manman was now wearing. It was the color that attracted her: hunter green was perfect for the task at hand.

Armed with sandwiches and a thermos of lemonade, we marched out of the house and headed north toward

Port-au-Prince. When we reached our destination, Manman was not surprised by the multitude already in line. "The enemy's camp is crowded, as usual," she sighed.

The people there generated a stifling heat that was exacerbated by the rising sun. A sea of bobbing heads glistened with sweat. Damp clothing stuck to faceless bodies that jostled for space, pushing and shoving, squeezing one behind the other, like the pods inside a pomegranate. Everyone wanted a chance to see the Angel of Mercy in person.

"*I want you to form two groups,*" a disembodied voice boomed through a megaphone. "*If you have a letter that says your appointment is today, stand on my right. If you do not have a letter with your appointment date, stand on my left.*"

From our position in the crowd, Manman could not discern where the speaker's right or left was. She did what she'd always done: joined the line with fewer people in it, the line where no one was hurling curses at the sky and spitting angrily on the pavement.

"Get out of my way! Move! Padon kò-w!" The crowd scattered, as if shots had been fired. Men and women shoved and elbowed one another roughly, as if they were fighting for their lives. "Make way! Make way!"

Like flour in a sieve, the bulk of the crowd sifted through one side and a few lumps remained on the other. Manman secured my hand in hers, pulling me toward the lumps that remained in the sieve. Someone from the opposite side yelled something about having an appointment but not the letter to prove it.

"*Then you do not have an appointment,*" the voice in the megaphone replied in Creole. "*And if you do not have one, I suggest you go home and wait for it to arrive in the mail.*"

"The mail!" a man howled. An explosion of laughter ensued. "We have mail in Haiti now?" Everyone, even Manman, laughed.

When the voice in the megaphone said, *"Or you can all go home and use your passports as kindling,"* a heavy silence fell on the crowd. The sea of bobbing heads had been parted by the powerful gatekeeper. Only a select few would have the chance to hope and plead and cry today.

Just as the moon had made way for the sun earlier, the gatekeeper stepped aside and let us in. Manman, in her hunter-green battle gear, did not get a chance to wield any of the weapons she brought along: a wedding picture with my father in that too-big suit, a snapshot of my sisters with tear-stained faces, another picture of my father looking particularly lonely in the faraway country where heavy woolen clothing was too often necessary.

The gargantuan being I expected to see was a bespectacled little man in charcoal-colored slacks, starched white shirt, suspenders that made an X on his back, and flip-flops that slapped the marble floor with each seemingly directionless step. His skin was the color of a dried corn husk—not quite yellow, not quite beige. He was not white like a page in my composition notebook, but everyone called him "Blan" just the same. His eyes were the blue of waters too deep to swim in. Deep like that place in the ocean from which people seldom returned. But his bottomless-blue eyes were not interested in drowning us today.

With a sweeping motion of his arms, the consul invited us into his office. Perhaps he had met his secret quota of humiliation for the day. Perhaps his hands ached from crushing family after family with his *Appli-*

cation Denied stamp. Perhaps he had grown tired of telling mothers and children to try again in six months or a year. Perhaps my green dress brought us good luck. "It was those psalms," Manman later declared. "They worked like magic!"

The consul signed Manman's papers hastily, as if some unseen hand were guiding his, forcing him to write his full name here, put his initials there, stamp that coveted seal of miracles in all the necessary places. Manman could not snatch the documents out of his hands fast enough. Within days we would be in an airplane, flying toward the unknown. I would see my father again for the first time in a decade. I had forgotten everything I was supposed to remember about him; everything except the name by which I would never be allowed to call him: Frisner Desormeau.

Manman was beside herself with happiness. She had her hair done, her nails and toes painted victory red. She would be with Papa again for the first time in much too long. As the day of our departure approached, a broader smile than usual skipped on her lips. The faraway look that had been in her eyes since the day Papa left gained greater distance, like a speedboat disappearing beyond the horizon. Manman's dreamy eyes followed the speedboat that held her future, hoping that it would not fall from the flat edge where the sun rises out of the sea.

STRANGE FRUIT

Manman wrapped ripe sweetsop in the prettiest nightgown she owned. She tucked the bundle in a corner of her carry-on bag under the most delicate panties I'd ever seen. She would surprise Frisner with those: the fruit, the nightgown, and the panties. He would be grateful. He would wonder how in God's name he survived without her for so long. How had he lived without her always thinking of him, always bringing him things like the only fruit in the world that had the power to melt his heart! Their happily-ever-after would resume with the first bite.

Manman had heard of people's fruit being tossed out by customs inspectors on the other side, but was certain that no one would bother hers. The nightgown and delicate panties were parts of a brilliant strategy: no stranger with an ounce of decency would touch a woman's underwear. Manman swore that her sweetsop would be as safe as a *ja* of gold buried under an unmarked tree in an orchard. No one would discover them. In a few hours, Frisner would taste all things past, present, and future in the succulent pulp.

My little sisters, Karine and Marjorie, daydreamed about the joys New York would bring: pretty dresses, new shoes, new ribbons for their hair, a doll like the one that disappeared from the upstairs bedroom. There would be candy by the ton. Life would be fun, fun, fun!

I daydreamed about what I would do once I reached New York too. I would find Yseult Joseph, my best friend, who was living there now. We would mend our friendship like the hem of a good dress that got caught in a thorn bush. We would patch the holes time created between us. We would be as close as we had been before she went away. We would be inseparable; this time forever.

I wrapped the six oslè I owned in a handkerchief and put them in the small purse that contained all the possessions Manman said I could take with me to the new country. Yseult and I would play oslè again.

Going to New York was like dying. We could not take most of our belongings with us.

On the night before we left, Manman gave away our dining table, the tablecloth, our dishes (even the good ones), our spoons, and every last grain of rice, sugar, and salt in the pantry. She gave away our pillows, the sheets on the bed, and the bed itself. Manman said we wouldn't need those old things. She said we would have new lives and new possessions to go with them.

Manman could not wait to reach New York. She could not wait to see Frisner again. She'd petitioned the consul in Port-au-Prince for years, begging him to approve her application. "My children need their father," she told him as tears leaked out of her eyes. She was overjoyed when the plane finally landed at JFK.

The worry lines that had been permanent fixtures on her face vanished. But when the cruel inspector at customs went through her carry-on bag and did the unthinkable, the lines instantly returned.

The inspector's trained nose had gone straight to the corner of Manman's bag where she'd hidden the sweetsop. He reached into the bag and removed her delicate panties—with a gloved pincer grip, as if they were soiled. He pulled Manman's pretty nightgown out of the bag, shaking the silk away from his body as if it were an animal that needed to be quarantined. The sweetsop Manman attempted to smuggle rolled out onto the table and stared back at her. Her secret had been revealed. The inspector's eyes accused her of an unspeakable crime. He did not ask questions. He did not have time to prosecute and punish her properly.

Dump the funny-looking crap and keep moving. There were thousands of bags to look through before his shift would end. Hundreds of strange fruit to throw into trash bins. "Next." The inspector's voice matched the fierce look in his eyes.

"Please, please," Manman said, but what the man heard was "Tanpri souple. Pa jete sa yo." Those words, like the fruit he'd gotten rid of, were foreign to him. They meant nothing.

Manman eyed the man and the garbage bin with equal disdain. Her joy had curdled. Something inside her had shifted. Something within her was now running and screaming like a child lost in dense woods. She'd made a mistake. Now that she was at the finish line, she realized that the race was fixed; she was bound to lose. Regret flooded her eyes when Frisner ran toward her with arms wide open.

Manman continued to cry when Frisner drove us to

the colossal building that would become our new home. She cried when we walked out of the car and took an elevator for the first time in our lives. She cried when the elevator's door slid open noisily and a corridor stretched out before us like a highway with carpet on it. The air smelled of thyme and rice pudding and cinnamon tea and burnt black beans and ginger cookies and strong coffee and beef stew with curry in it. Loud voices behind the black metal doors spoke languages I did not recognize. Manman continued to cry.

She cried as Frisner charged ahead and we followed him like ducklings. She cried as we walked past door after door after door on either side of the wide, carpeted highway. "Each door has a private home behind it," Frisner offered. "Some have two, three, even four bedrooms."

"Each one has a kitchen?" Karine's voice bounced off the walls.

"Each one," Frisner said without turning around. He would match our voices to our faces later.

"What about a latrine?" Marjorie had a pinched look on her face. She must have forgotten to relieve herself for days.

The excitement of going to New York had nearly consumed all of us. Karine could not bring herself to eat a bite of food; my own eyes refused to stay shut at night for more than a few minutes at a time.

"Where is the latrine?" Marjorie asked with even more urgency.

"Inside our apartment. Each apartment has its own toilet." Frisner enunciated the word *toilet* carefully, letting us know that latrines—and all of their filthy, deep-in-the-woods connotations—belonged in the other world, not here. Frisner was careful not to call any of us by name. Perhaps he had forgotten them. Perhaps he could not recall Manman's name either. Everything was *chérie* this and *sweetheart* that. Karine and Marjorie looked at each other and shrugged.

Frisner produced a large ring with a collection of keys on it. He jingled the keys theatrically in midair, telling us—without words—that only men of great importance could be trusted with so many keys.

"Welcome home, my love, my children!" Frisner's face was arranged in a proud grin. But Manman missed both the "Welcome home" and the "my love" parts. The heartless man at the airport had thrown out a piece of her with the sweetsop. Both were now in a dump somewhere, rotting. Manman could not explain her loss to anyone, not to Frisner and certainly not to me.

When, after several months, the disappearance of Manman's beloved tropical fruit still brought tears to her eyes, she opened her mouth and spat out the words that had simmered inside her all along: "I want to go back."

"Kisa?" Frisner was incredulous. "You must be sick."

"This country is for giants," Manman explained with a desperate edge in her voice. "The buildings are too big. The streets are too wide. The stores are too bright. The lights are never off. The people never sleep. I feel like a grasshopper here. Vulnerable. An ant is what I feel like. I don't belong in this place."

The city intimidated Manman. The lights that were never turned off illuminated things she wished she did not have to see: ladies in neon shorts beckoning strangers and servicing them behind the bushes three stories below our living room window. But I needed those lights to shine eternally so I could find my friend Yseult Joseph.

Manman thought the artificially lit nights were terrifying. Back on the island, nighttime was as it was meant to be: dark. People became shadows at night, just as they were supposed to. Good shadows went home, bolted their doors, read the Bible, and slept. Bad shadows shed their skin, grew horns, tails, and hooves, and grazed like stray goats; they roamed city streets and the countryside, wreaking havoc until the soft blue light just before dawn. New York, Manman said, was supposed to be different. The people were supposed to be sophisticated. They were supposed to have a sense of occasion. They were supposed to sleep at night.

The click-clicking of high heels on the pavement below our window was terrifying. The ladies strutting like seagulls along the water's edge, day and night, were worse than those demons that used to gather on rooftops to inventory the souls of homeless children in Port-au-Prince. The ladies kept Manman awake at night. New York was an unnatural place, she concluded, an open grave with dirt and snow piled high on either side. She wanted to fly back toward the familiar island sun and never return.

"I brought you out of there and now you want to go back!" Frisner was stunned. "If you leave New York . . . I swear . . ." He did not have to say the rest. *If you leave now, we're done, through, over, divorced.* "You hated your life there," he reminded her. "Have you forgotten how much you couldn't wait to leave?"

"I was happy!" I could not believe Manman uttered those words. If anyone was happy in Haiti, it was me.

Unhappiness came only when a certain someone made me read fifty thousand psalms when I was too tired to do anything but close my eyes and dream about Yseult Joseph. Until Yseult got on a plane and left me without a best friend, I was the happiest person on the island, wasn't I? She used to come to my house every day after school. We'd eat mangoes and sweetsop until our stomachs ached. We kept our eyes on the doll in the upstairs room, and she never bothered us, did she? The doll was happy too, wasn't she? Until she heard all that talk about us going to New York. It was only then that she left her cobweb-ridden high chair and was never seen again.

Frisner was supposed to quiver with joy upon meeting the girls he'd fathered but left behind for Manman to raise on her own. Reality in the form of indifference erased that thought and filled Manman's mouth with a taste so sour that to this day she cannot help but be bitter.

He was nowhere near thrilled to rediscover the particulars of full-time fatherhood.

Taking care of himself hadn't been so expensive and time-consuming. (A few kind women picked up the slack here and there—cooking warm meals, ironing sheets that didn't need it.) Now, in addition to the landlord demanding to be paid, the grocer, the doctor, the dentist, and the pharmacist also wanted money. Even the washing machines at the laundromat didn't care if there was only a nickel left to be split five ways. *Feed me or wear filthy clothes*, they hummed.

Frisner's unexpected announcement came one payday after he counted the change that was left once all the bills were paid. "Children are like industrial-strength juicers," he said. Manman listened quietly. "By the time they're done with us, we won't have any pulp left. But we could have a good life, if we sent them back. They'd be fine down there. They're young. They'd go back to school. A year's tuition costs less than what I spend on food in a single week. We could have a happy life, you and me. This country isn't good for children anyway. Especially girls. What do you say, chérie?"

Manman was too stunned to answer right away. After a few minutes of deliberation she said, "Flora is the oldest. I suppose we could send her back."

"On top of that," Frisner went on contemptuously, unaware that Manman had made up her mind about what she would do, "there are laws in this country that dictate what we can and can't do inside our own house. If you step out of line, your own children can crush you like the grasshopper you keep talking about. If they don't feel like doing what you tell them, they can just pick up the phone and off to jail you go to eat your meals with rapists and murderers."

Manman had heard rumors about American children having their parents arrested for setting them straight. "Not Haitian children," Manman said. "My Karine and Marjorie would never."

"Children are the real giants in this country," Frisner half-joked. "They're expensive as hell to keep. And they have rights! In Haiti you can erase them like mistakes on a sheet of paper. Do anything you want with them. It's not like that here. You look at them wrong and an avalanche of trouble will tumble down on you. How many times, back on the island, did someone give away an unwanted child to a neighbor, a friend, a stranger? You could take a kid to the countryside and leave him there like a bag of old clothes. Who would care? There are so many abandoned kids on the island, who could count them all? Try any of that here. Try dropping them off somewhere and see what happens. Someone is always watching." Frisner was laughing and slapping his knees.

Manman sucked her teeth. She was repulsed by his words, however true they were. "Karine and Marjorie would never hurt us," she maintained.

"We could have a nice life here," Frisner reiterated. "You and me."

"If I stay, my girls stay with me."

"You'll regret it," Frisner snapped.

He was no longer laughing. No longer listening. He did not hear the compromise: "Flora, on the other hand, would get along just fine without us. In fact, the sooner we send her back . . ."

"To hell with all this," Frisner said, and slammed the door behind him.

He returned many hours later. A woman's perfume was mingled up with the smell of engine grease embedded in his woolen jacket. The perfume filled every inch of the apartment, daring us to try and ignore it. Daring Manman to state the obvious: *This is not Joie de Vivre. This is not my perfume.*

Manman soon found a solution to Frisner's problem (the high cost of raising a family) and hers (the click-clicking of the prostitutes' heels on the pavement below our window). She took a factory job working from sundown to sunup. She would silence the ladies' heels as well as Frisner's pleas to toss her girls back to the island like unwanted catch into the sea.

Frisner now walked around the apartment with his head down all the time, sulking like a boy who could not find his favorite toy. Manman had traded him in for a job and was punching a time clock at the exact moment when they were supposed to slip into bed together. He took solace in endowing himself with the gift of prophecy. "You're wrong," he told Manman angrily one morning upon picking her up from the factory. "You're very wrong: New York won't crush me like some little grasshopper. But it will crush you. And it will make your daughters walk the streets, day and night. It will turn all of them into bouzen. Whores. Mark my words."

"Not my Karine and Marjorie," Manman fired back. "Those girls take after me. Flora has too much of your blood in her veins. She looks and acts just like you. If you say New York will turn her into a bouzen, who would I be to disagree?"

FLORA DESORMEAU

Sister Bernadête doesn't want me to sit next to Yseult, but she doesn't want me near the other girls in class either. "You'll contaminate them," the nun says. I prefer to be near Yseult; she's my right arm. She lets me copy the pages I need to memorize for the next day's recitations.

"*La Reine Anacaona fut enchaînée.*" Yseult is standing in front of the class now, reciting her history homework. "*Anacaona, the queen, was captured and taken to Santo Domingo. She was hung at the public square.*"

"Very good," Sister Bernadête says. "Very good" that the queen was captured and hung, or "Very good" that Yseult recited the lesson perfectly? Sister Bernadête smiles. The irony of it all: a citizen of the old mother country teaching Haitian children about history.

Yseult curtsies before returning to the seat next to me. I am not surprised when Sister Bernadête calls me next. I make my way to the front of the class and begin to recite the part about the *Indiens* being exterminated by a handful of Spaniards.

"When did the first blacks arrive in Haiti?" Sister Bernadête likes to try and confuse me. Her question has nothing to do with my recitation. And she knows I'm not good with dates.

"1503," I tell her.

A mixture of disappointment and surprise flashes across her face. "Go to your seat," she says in French. "And keep your mouth shut."

"Keep *your* mouth shut," someone mimics the nun.

"Who spoke?" Sister Bernadête wants to know.

"Yseult Joseph," the other girls in class chorus.

Sister Bernadête is not convinced. "Flora Desormeau, what did you say?"

I shake my head. "Nothing." I know what's coming.

"Both of you," the nun says to Yseult and me, "to the wall. On your knees. Now!"

"Dog shit," Yseult mumbles under her breath, but I hear her clearly.

"Dog shit," I mumble under my breath too.

"You two little piglets are disrupting my class!" Sister Bernadête shrieks, shaking menacing fists. "Face the wall, dumb mules. I don't want to look at monkey faces anymore today." The other girls in class cover their mouths as they laugh.

Sister Bernadête's face is a fluffy pink pillow with big blue buttons for eyes. Her cheeks are red like the roses that grow around the grotto with the statue of the Virgin in it. Her lips are communion-wafer thin. Her large round eyeglasses make her head look like a full moon.

"Imbéciles," she says. "Do not move until I tell you otherwise."

Yseult and I have served this sentence countless times. Our knees are best friends with the cracked cement floor.

"C'est vraiment dégoûtant!" The nun's French is so

beautiful. It doesn't even sound like she's insulting us; her French is like a song—a fierce and passionate song overflowing with regret. Nostalgia.

"Imbéciles!" Yseult does her best imitation of the nun's accent. My "C'est vraiment dégoûtant" doesn't come close to sounding as pretty as Sister Bernadête's.

Yseult and I practiced our French for years, but we're nowhere near Sister Bernadête's native-speaker timbre. The easy, unforced cadence will never dance off our tongues as it does hers.

The other girls in class, the ones who speak to their parents and their maids in French, they'll sound like Sister Bernadête one day. Some of them already do. Not us. Yseult and I speak only Creole with each other and at home. Now, we gladly face the wall. The nun doesn't realize that this punishment is sweeter to us than a hundred tito candy sticks rolled up into one. If she had any idea how much we loved it, she would think of something else. Of course, we never let on that we're happy to stay on our knees for hours, watching the goings-on in the hotel below.

"Idiots!" The nun throws in one last insult in her pretty French.

Yseult and I look at each other and smile again. Now we have complete access to the tourists behind Cabane Choucoune's tall wrought-iron gates. We are like angels watching over them, seeing everything they do.

Cabane Choucoune is exactly one hundred and twenty-six paces away from the school. But from our position in the classroom, it may as well be right below our window.

Even though the tourists never vary their routine,

the scene around the pool is always worth Sister Bernadête's wrath. When they're not splashing around, the men-tourists stretch out under the sun until their backs turn boiled-lobster red. Then they flip over and do the same to their front sides. The women-tourists wear enormous hats and bathing suits emblazoned with giant sunflowers and ferns. There aren't any children-tourists. Maybe tourists don't like children.

Maybe children don't like to be tourists. Even if they did, Manman says, Cabane Choucoune isn't a place for kids.

The tourist-wives, in their enormous hats, sit at the edge of the pool, reading magazines and dipping painted toes into the sea-blue water. Sun-seared servers, in head-to-toe karabela accented with yards of multicolored ruffles, shuffle in and out of a revolving door. Each one balances a tray heaped with glasses that have little umbrellas in them (to keep the drinks from getting wet, should all that splashing around in the pool get out of control).

The little umbrellas are pretty, but the tourists pull them out of their glasses as soon as they snatch them off the servers' trays. They destroy the pretty umbrellas while they sip their drinks. They break the tiny wooden poles, the ribs, and then they crush the colorful paper covers between their fingers.

The house where I live is fifty-three paces from Cabane Choucoune. I can see the sweetsop trees in our yard from Sister Bernadête's classroom. Our house is a two-story A-frame with slender windows that have white shutters on either side. The floor creaks. Otherwise it is a very quiet house. The other place where we used to live was not quiet at all. We had to leave it after Papa went to New York. Manman could not live there with Papa gone. She said a bad spirit moved in the day he left. The bad spirit refused to let her sleep at night. It was in the air, under the floorboards, behind the walls, on the roof, but mostly inside Manman's head.

Manman likes our new house better. The staircase that leads upstairs curves like a capital S. The banister looks like it belongs in a fairy tale. The wraparound porch is a good place to sit and watch hummingbirds flutter their wings as they feed on soft blossoms. The pantry is large enough for a flock of chickens, but only one lives in there. We bring her in at night from the yard. She gives us one egg every morning.

There are two bedrooms upstairs, but we occupy only one. The other stays locked all the time. The land-lord says he lost the key to that door. We cannot open it. A doll lives in the locked bedroom. She sits in a high chair. Her hair glistens in the sunlight that streams in through a hole in the roof. Her lips are like a dried rosebud. Her face is pudgy, round, and pink like Sister Bernadête's.

"You can almost see the doll room from here," I whisper to Yseult.

"Shut up, little serpents!" the nun yells.

I wait for Sister Bernadête to choose another animal in her menagerie of insults, but she does not. Her jowls shake and she scrunches up her lips hard as if she's try-ing to keep the words she's not allowed to speak from slipping out. I turn my attention back to Cabane Chou-coune. The tourists continue to bake themselves. The servers have fresh drinks on their trays. I try to count the little umbrellas. The tourists crush them even faster now.

When the bell rings, Sister Bernadête exhales loudly. "Good riddance, little bats."

Yseult and I bolt out of the classroom like the African gazelles we read about in geography class.

Yvela is outside, as usual, waiting. She's a few months older than Yseult and I, but looks much older. Yseult and I hold hands and skip down the street to my house. Our feet barely touch the ground. Yvela runs behind us.

Naturally, we stop by Cabane Choucoune and peep through the wrought-iron gate that separates the hotel from the rest of the island. The tourists are still baking themselves and dipping their toes in the sparkling water. The servers are still shuffling in and out of the revolving door with an assortment of drinks on their trays.

"One day," Yseult says, "I'll come to Cabane Choucoune and dip my toes in the pool too. I'll sip drinks with umbrellas in them and have lots of fun too. One day I'll wear a large hat and sunglasses that hide my eyes. One day I'll wear a bathing suit with flowers on it too. One day after I become a famous artist . . . One day . . . Maybe after I go to New York and my paintings are in every gallery in the world and I become rich and beautiful like the tourist wives. One day."

Yvela laughs and says, "Woy, pitit! You have a better chance of wearing that ruffled skirt and serving the tourists their drinks."

"Close your stinky snout," Yseult snaps, and Yvela's face looks fifty years older. "When I grow up, I'll be rich and beautiful. And I will come to Cabane Choucoune and do as I please. Yvela Germain, you'll be the one wearing the servant's skirt. You'll be the one bringing me whatever I ask. You'll be my personal rèstavèk—just like you are now."

"What about Flora?" Yvela has a smirk on her face. Her young mistress could dream a great future for herself, but what would she predict for her friend? "What is Flora going to do while you're busy being rich and beautiful and so on?"

"Flora is my best friend," Yseult retorts. "We'll be together. Always. Naturally, when I come to Cabane Choucoune, she'll be with me."

Yvela cups her hands over her rows of cracked, rust-colored teeth and giggles. "She'll take my place then!"

I pretend not to hear. Yseult is a great artist. She sketches everything she sees and makes them look better than they are in real life. She's sketched me a thousand times and managed to make me look presentable.

Yseult always says she will be a great artist one day; I believe her. As for me, I don't know what I'll be when I grow up. Maybe I'll learn to make school uniforms and wedding gowns for ladies who don't know how. Maybe I'll die before I become anything. Who knows? But if Yseult tells me that we'll come back to Cabane Choucoune together one day to be as carefree as the tourist-wives, then that's exactly what will happen.

"Yseult Joseph," Yvela screams, "let's go before your manman sends the Tonton Macoutes after me."

"Manman doesn't care what time I get home anymore!" Yseult shouts back, taking my hand in hers. "Flora and I will play oslè for as long as we want. You can take me home afterward."

Yvela scratches her head while mumbling something under her breath.

When we reach my house, we take off our shoes and sit on the porch. I press the soles of my feet against Yseult's. There's a diamond-shaped space between us. Our skirts are bunched up and tucked under our thighs.

Yseult throws the first round of oslè. We use real goat joints, not those slime-green plastic jacks that some of the girls whose mothers live in New York send them. She throws one of the oslè high above her head. "Un do," she says and picks one up from the floor. "Deux do." She picks up two. "Trois do . . ." She drops one of the oslè and grunts. It's now my turn. "Yvela, fetch my things."

Yvela brings Yseult her sketchbook and a pencil. Yseult stares at my face while her right hand moves swiftly on the paper. She shows me her creation a few moments later: my eyes now have a mountain range in them.

I can play oslè for hours without losing a turn. Yseult doesn't mind. She can sketch for hours without stopping. She draws one of the mango trees with ripe fruit hanging from its limbs. "Yvela," Yseult says, "get us a couple of good ones from that tree."

Yvela scales the tree like a boy. Her scarred knees cling to the bark. Yseult sketches Yvela's face and gives her the body of a zandolit—a lizard. Yvela's grip is firm as she pulls herself higher and higher. "Come get them," Yvela calls out.

Yseult and I run toward the tree to catch the fruit in our skirts, lest they fall on the ground and burst. When Yvela climbs back down, we sit together and eat until we're full.

"Wait for me here," Yseult tells Yvela.

"What else would I do?" Yvela sucks her teeth.

"Keep showing off," Yseult says. "See if I don't tell Manman. See if she doesn't pull out what's left of your brown teeth."

Yvela makes the sign of the cross on her lips. "Pardon me," she responds.

"I want to see," Yseult says as she takes my hand. She wants to go upstairs every time she comes to my house after school, especially when Manman is not here.

"Where is she?" Yseult squints as she peeps through the keyhole. "Where is the doll?"

"I don't know," I tell her. I look through the keyhole too. The high chair is there, but the doll is not. "Stay with me."

"I can't," Yseult answers quickly. Her eyes dart about. She runs down the stairs.

"I don't want to be alone," I tell her.

I have to go, she says without words. Just her eyes.

When we reach the porch, Yseult takes Yvela's hand and runs away.

Madan Casseus watches me when Manman is away. She won't get here until dark. I try not to think about the missing doll. I try not to think about anything at all.

Manman went to the leaves doctor's compound again. She took Karine and Marjorie with her. Manman took me to the leaves doctor once, but the man said I was different from the other girls somehow and did not need special protection against bad spirits. (Manman is afraid the bad spirit might follow her to our new house. The leaves doctor concocts a special lotion that's supposed to keep all bad spirits away.)

To get to the leaves doctor's compound, you have to start walking before the sun even thinks about rising. Walk for a long time, past a cemetery teeming with stray goats and graves heaped with food and candle wax. Go through the marketplace where vendors haggle in a singsong that tells you you're a long way from Port-au-Prince. Cross a valley full of bones that crumble under your feet. Pray that the scorpions scurrying on the blistering rocks don't sting you. Walk some more until you see the statue of Fatima nestled in the shimmering mosaic grotto on the other side of a little stream. Cross the little stream, then stop. Stop at the grotto; everyone does. Kiss Fatima's feet three times. Seven, if the line behind you isn't too long. Then walk up a mountain that's so high it takes hours to reach the top. When you do reach the top, sit down and rest awhile before starting down the other side. The leaves doctor's compound is visible from that distance, but you won't reach his front door until it's so dark that you'll think you're blind. But you're not blind because your eyes will catch the glow of a bald-headed lamp that'll draw your shadow into the house long before you reach it. When Manman goes to the leaves doctor's compound, she stays for several days so that he has plenty of time to do whatever it is she's convinced he can do.

Since Madan Casseus won't get here until after dark, I'll wait for her on the porch. When I hear her donkey approaching, I'll pretend to be asleep. She'll shake my shoulders gently and tell me to come inside. *Young girl, children mustn't sit outside by themselves.*

We'll go inside. She'll offer me some of the food that the taptap drivers did not buy from her. I'll take some fried plantain and spicy blood pudding. Then Madan Casseus will make me take off my school uniform and iron the wrinkles out of it. She'll make me wash my feet in the basin before going to bed. I'll put on my night-gown while she bolts the front door. She'll tell me to pray for my mother and sisters. "Priye pou Manman-w, pitit. Pray for them." I'll kneel down by the bed. Cross myself. Recite the Our Father. Madan Casseus will re-cite the Our Father along with me. "Good night," she'll say. "Dream about butterflies and rainbows."

"Good night," I'll say. "Dream about butterflies and rainbows too."

In the morning, Madan Casseus will saddle the don-key and ride down to Kalfou Djoumbala. She'll spend the day there, selling food to famished taptap drivers and their passengers. I won't see her again until after dark.

In the morning, I will wait for Yseult to stop by on her way to school. We'll run together, hand in hand. Yvela will carry Yseult's bags as she follows us. She'll leave only after the nun locks the gate.

Yseult and I will stand one behind the other to pledge our undying love for our nation and her flag. We'll throw our voices high when we sing our national anthem.

Yseult's voice will sound pretty. Her French will sound better when it's mixed up with the other girls', the ones who speak it even when no one is listening. *"Marchons unis! Marchons unis! In our midst there are no traitors . . ."*

Afterward, we'll go to Sister Bernadête's class and hope that she banishes us to the back of the room again. At lunchtime, we'll eat quickly. Afterward, we'll play La Ronde with the only other girls in school we like: Marie Lourdes Jean, Caroline Saint Louis, and Elizabeth

Lafrance. We'll stomp our feet and sing our favorite La Ronde song which is also an old history lesson about Napoléon Bonaparte and Henri Christophe, "*Commandant, Commandant du Cap!*"

If there's still time before our next class we'll play Good Underwear. We'll lower our voices so that the nuns don't hear. One girl will step inside the circle and twirl around as fast as she can. We will inspect her underwear. If there are holes, we will laugh her out of the circle. If the elastic around the thighs is frayed, we will laugh her out of the circle. If the girl is bashful and refuses to spin around, we will pull her out of the circle and push someone else in. No one will have to push Yseult in. Playing Good Underwear is her second favorite thing in life. Yseult's panties are the best. Her papa sends them from New York. My panties are not so bad today. When it's my turn inside the circle, I'll spin like a hurricane whipping though palm fronds. I'll spin and spin while the other girls cheer: "Sak pa vire kilòt yo gen twou!" Spin, spin. Show us your good underwear.

A NEW LIFE

There's a roach on the patch of ceiling directly above my bed. I gather the blanket around me, leaving only a slit to watch its whereabouts.

Across the room, my sisters are sprawled out on the double bed they share. Karine is reading one of her mystery novels. Marjorie, the youngest, is injecting her brain with another dose of Daffy Duck.

Brooke Shields pops up on the screen, smiling a dazzling smile and winking her pretty-baby eyes. "Nothing comes between me and my Calvins," she coos, just as another roach starts to stroll across her face. Killing it would cut into Marjorie's cartoon time, so she pardons the roach the way President Reagan pardoned the White House turkey last Thanksgiving.

When we hear the rattle of keys on the other side of the bedroom wall, Karine cringes and shoves the paperback under her pillow. Marjorie jumps from under the sheets as if a scorpion had stung her. She turns off the TV, whispering: "Shit. Shit. Shit." My hands have a sudden dampness in them. The knot in my stomach tightens at the sound of my father's grunts.

"Frisner is here," Karine announces, as if no one else could tell.

I take a final look at the roach on the ceiling before switching off the lamp next to my bed. The room is silent now; everything is black. In the world inside my head, the sun is sizzling. I'm holding Yseult Joseph's right hand in mine. We're playing the Good Underwear game, singing, "*Sak pa vire kilòt yo gen twou!*" Caroline Saint Louis, Marie Lourdes Jean, and Elizabeth Lafrance are all there—in my old school yard. The nuns are in the upstairs chapel, saying their noonday prayers. Sister Bernadêtte cannot see us now. We're free to spin as wildly as we please; free to play the forbidden Good Underwear game.

Caroline steps into the circle and starts twirling. She twirls faster and faster. Her skirt flies up to her waist. Her panties are pink with fraying white ruffles around her skinny thighs. "*Kilòt ou gen twou. Your panties have holes,*" we chant and laugh until she stumbles out of the circle, ashamed but not so consumed that she cannot continue to play. Her face glistens with perspiration.

Yseult lets go of my hand and leaps into the circle. Her braids flap up and down. The white ribbons hang loose—the bows undone. She sings as she twirls. Her panties are perfect: No holes. No fraying lace.

Yseult staggers in my direction, singing: "*Sak pa vire kilòt yo gen twou.*" It's my turn to step into the circle. I spin around so fast that the girls' faces become one big blur as the sun melts a rainbow in the sky and everything turns black and I fall down on the bed with the roach on the patch of ceiling directly above my head.

The front door squeaks. The deadbolt clicks. The chain lock slips into place. Frisner makes his way in the dark stealthily, hoping to catch us doing one of the fifty billion things we're not permitted to do.

He's on the other side of the bedroom door now, one ear pressed against the flaking mustard-colored paint, hoping to hear something—anything to confirm his suspicion that America damages girls.

I cannot see Frisner's grease-stained fingers reaching through the hole where the doorknob used to be, but I know the movement just the same. (Frisner removed that doorknob when we moved into the apartment. *Good girls don't need locks on their doors*, he'd said.)

Frisner is in our bedroom now, waiting, like the demon Sister Bernadête always warned us about. Her beautiful French lilt had done nothing to mask the ugliness of the name—God's disobedient child sentenced to an eternal time-out.

I cannot see Frisner's face, but I know that look on it—the look of someone condemned to spend eternity in a dingy apartment that's arctic cold in the winter and infernal during the summer months. I imagine him cocking his head to the side as if there were horns jutting out of his scalp, weighing him down.

Frisner grunts again. He is glad to be home, but loathes this cramped space. If Manman would only agree to send us back to Haiti, his lifestyle would improve significantly. The room my sisters and I sleep in would be used as the dining room it was meant to be. The walk-in closet which he sleeps in could be used as a closet again. If only Manman would agree to send us back, his weekly paycheck wouldn't have to stretch so far. He could put a few dollars away. Maybe take a vacation one of these years. He could go to Mexico and France—countries he loves without knowing why.

I can feel his eyes trying to adjust to the darkness.

The narrow aisle between our beds is his personal virgin forest this time of night. He is the explorer who will trample upon the lush grounds. He is the hunter waiting for the slightest movement, a rustling of leaves. And then he will strike.

I hold my breath. Frisner knows I'm only pretending to be asleep, but he does not say a word. A good hunter keeps his mouth shut. A good hunter does not make a sound. After a few minutes of silence, he pounds his way to his bedroom.

Manman works nights at the factory across town. They don't sleep together anymore.

In the morning when I wake up, the first thing I see is that official-looking letter which Mrs. Williams, my American History teacher, sent to my parents. Frisner taped it on the wall next to my bed, daring me to remove it.

Mrs. Williams's letter says I am in danger of failing her class. Frisner responded to it by threatening to send me back to the island if I don't get an A. He is convinced my brain is packed tight with thoughts about boys and sex.

"One day some guy's going to give you what you're after," Frisner likes to say. "When he does, I will not save you from it. You'll be on your own then." Manman agrees with him. This is why she makes me come straight home from school every day.

From noon to four thirty, Monday through Friday, Manman watches *Ryan's Hope*, *All My Children*, *One Life to Live*, *General Hospital*, and *The Edge of Night*. "You girls better be home before *The Edge of Night* ends," she tells us, "or I'll let your papa know that you're turning American. He'll fix you before the transformation is complete."

Sometimes Manman lifts up her arms and cries out, "Woy, Bon Dye! Why did You curse me with a heap of girls? Why didn't You give me sons instead? Boys get a girl pregnant, but you can't prove they were even in the same room. Girls carry the proof in their bellies for the world to see."

Frisner's tongue is a knot when Manman mourns her lot. Maybe that's because he remembers causing a young girl's belly to swell with proof once. To make things right, he married that girl: Manman wore a white dress that stretched over my unborn body and a half-happy, half-sad look in her eyes. Frisner wore a black suit—the kind they bury accident victims in.

An uninvited guest, Hurricane Flora, crashed their wedding, reversing their chance at happiness. Tempestuous winds nearly tore the roof off the church before the priest could pronounce them husband and wife. The relentless downpour that accompanied Flora turned the ground into a reddish paste that coated the bride's pretty shoes. The black-and-white photographs captured her annoyance. Her lips stayed pursed. Manman would have defeated the force that caused the hurricane—if only it had a face.

I was born forty days after the wedding and named for the hurricane that destroyed Manman's magical moment on its way to killing thousands on the island. Karine came twelve months later, Marjorie twelve months after that. If Frisner had not left for the United States, there would have been more *proof* swelling up Manman's belly. But he stayed away. We did not see him again for almost a decade.

Nine years and nine months later, we received an appointment to see the consul at the American Embassy—for the thirteenth time. The man behaved as if he could not wait to scribble his name on the documents in Manman's hands.

"Congratulations," he said. "You and your children can be reunited with Mr. Desormeau at long last!"

Within days we were following Manman on a slippery tarmac bordered with mounds of snow. Frozen rain slapped our faces, causing Manman's eye shadow to run. Every strand of her freshly pressed hair balled up like little fists that sparred with one another. Nothing was left of her beautiful coiffure but the horse's tail pinned to the back of her head.

We've been in the States three years now and our daily routine never changes:

Frisner drives us to school in the morning, and picks Manman up from the factory on the way. When she gets in the car, she groans a reply to our collective *Bonjour*, then sets her head against the passenger-side window and falls asleep.

When we reach the school, we say, *Au revoir*, and kiss Manman on the cheek. We kiss Frisner too—though we don't like to. As soon as the crossing guard gives us permission, we bolt. Frisner takes Manman home before driving to the auto parts plant where he works.

The first thing I do once inside the school building is unravel the Flora-Desormeau-just-came-from-Haiti cornrows that Frisner makes me wear. The shiny blue boul gogo barrettes scream *newcomer*. I force my hair into a ponytail and trace around the shape of each eye with the black pencil I bought from Newberry's for ninety-nine cents. This doesn't make me feel like some Egyptian princess or anything, just different from the girl whose parents think she'll turn American and curdle like milk. I stop in the bathroom to wash off the eyeliner and redo the braids every afternoon before going back home.

Manman's daily routine never changes either. Once Frisner drops her off at the apartment, she sleeps until it's time for *Ryan's Hope*. She cooks, cleans, and does the ironing during the commercials.

By *All My Children*, the pot of rice is ready. Before *One Life to Live* ends, the goat meat is so tender it's sliding off the bone. By *General Hospital*, the apartment is guests-are-coming tidy. By then, Manman is also dressed and ready for work. Everything must be in its place before her favorite show begins. Nothing must disturb her when she settles down to watch the adventures of Luke and Laura, her favorite characters on *General Hospital*.

Manman expects us home at the beginning of *The Edge of Night*, the last soap opera of the day. If we're not there while the opening theme song is playing, she panics.

"New York is a terrible place to raise daughters," Manman tells Frisner. "Luke and Laura might have gotten married, but there's still plenty that's wrong with America."

"I'm tired of your TV people," Frisner responds.

"And I'm tired of the giants that like to step on grasshoppers, crushing them just for fun."

"You're not a grasshopper."

"I wasn't one in Haiti. I am one here. So are you."

Now, when Manman talks about the grasshopper and the giants, Frisner walks away. "You're the damn grasshopper!" he shouts in Creole.

On Saturdays, my sisters and I wipe off the layer of dust on the incomplete set of Encyclopedia Britannica. Manman catches up on some of the sleep she missed all week. Frisner fills the air with sentimental boleros and reminisces about God knows what. He turns the volume up so high you'd think Juan Gabriel and his band were in the living room with him, providing the soundtrack for his top-secret thoughts. He plays the same Spanish song all the time. I know the lyrics by heart. I had a kid at school translate: "*You are always on my mind . . .*"

When Frisner is done serenading the house with his sad song, he showers and shaves and piles on the Old Spice before driving to his girlfriend's house—the one who sends him love letters all the time. Manman wouldn't know what's in those letters even if Frisner left them on the kitchen table like place mats. Still, he keeps them locked in the small safe behind the couch.

I check that safe periodically, in case Frisner forgets to lock it like he did once.

That's how I found out that he has a couple of children by a seamstress back on the island. Those boys in the pictures look just like him: same forehead, same eyes, same nose, same teeth. I don't think Manman knows about Frisner's other family. But one look at those boys and his little secret would burst into flames and burn Manman down. There's a boy at school who looks just like Frisner. I wonder if he is my brother too.

Sundays we drive to Brooklyn to visit relatives who seldom visit us. If we go by way of the Holland Tunnel,

Manman tells Frisner to stop in Chinatown so that she can haggle with the street vendors like she used to in Port-au-Prince. If we head to the Lincoln Tunnel, which takes us to 42nd Street, Manman stares at the pimps in fur coats and hats as big and ornamented as cruise liners. She cringes when she sees the ladies in shimmering halter tops, up-to-here miniskirts, and thigh-high boots with stilts for heels. When Frisner sees those prostitutes, he says: "There goes Flora!" Manman usually nods in agreement.

Manman predicts it's only a matter of time before a pimp puts me to work. "Look at Bobbie Spencer on *General Hospital*," she says: "If a pimp can turn that pretty white girl into a bouzen, no girl child is safe in America."

When we drive past Times Square on the way to the Manhattan Bridge which spills onto Flatbush Avenue, I keep my eyes fixed on the Broadway theaters, searching for Yseult Joseph's name. Perhaps one day two cars will pull up at a red light at the same time. I'll be in one with my family, Yseult and her family will be in the other. We'll roll down the windows and scream our telephone numbers before the light changes. And then we'll be inseparable again. Like the wings of a hummingbird.

On the way home from school one afternoon, Tamara, my sometimes girlfriend, runs toward me, calling out: "Flora, Flora, Flora Desormeau, chérie. Attends moi!"

Tamara is Haitian, but tells everyone she's from Tahiti. Because she's a half-Syrian grimèl with silky-smooth, siwo myèl hair, the American kids have no trouble believing her. They'd believe her if she said she came from Pluto. Those American kids adore Miss Tahiti.

"Where are you going?" she asks in a forceful way. Yseult never spoke to me like that.

"Lakay mwen," I tell her.

Tamara pretends not to understand, but that girl speaks more Creole than all the fish vendors in Kwabo-sal put together.

"Home," I repeat in English.

"Let's go to the arcade," Tamara says in that same perfect French Sister Bernadête used to speak. Yseult wouldn't have asked me to go anywhere or do anything she knew I was not supposed to.

"I can't go to the arcade," I tell her. I don't say what Manman thinks of those places: *Only bad girls go to arcades—to look for boys who can't wait to put proof in their bellies. Only bad girls behave in such a way to make the world point fingers and disrespect the family that failed to raise them properly.*

"I can't go with you," I tell Tamara again, but the thought of playing a video game starts my heart racing.

"Are you scared?" she asks, laughing.

The Edge of Night is about to begin, I tell myself. If I'm not home by the time the opening theme song ends, Manman will call Frisner and a thousand tongues won't be enough to describe what he'll do to me.

"Flora!" Marjorie and Karine say my name as if it's a bad word. "It's three forty-five."

I'm too busy trying to solve the math problem in my head to answer: *General Hospital* ends in fifteen minutes. Manman has to leave for work in forty-five. How much time will I have to play if it takes five minutes to reach the arcade and fifteen minutes to walk home from there?

"Flora!"

"Tell Manman I had to stay after school to help the new teacher with something."

Karine and Marjorie shake their heads in disbelief. I wave them away.

"Tell Manman that Mr. E asked me to stay after school to help with a project for extra credit. Tell her anything. I'll be home before *The Edge of Night* ends."

"Ti fi?" Marjorie's eyes have a nervous look in them.

"You'll regret it!" Karine shouts.

Tamara and I run to the arcade.

The kid playing on a *Ms. Pac-Man* machine near the entrance gets the high score and writes his name in bold letters, letting everyone know about his accomplishment. He runs toward a group of boys standing around a pinball machine.

Now it's my turn to try and get a high score. I slip a quarter into the slot. The electronic jingle pulls me into a carnival of magical colors. Four ghosts with large eyes try to keep me from eating the cluster of cherries now inching away from the screen. Those cherries are worth a hundred points, so I move the joystick toward them, but the ghosts swarm me. I pump another quarter into the slot. The ghosts race toward me, trying to eliminate me before I score any points. I pump in another quarter. And another. And another. Tamara taps me on the shoulder.

"What?"

"It's five o'clock," she blurts out like it's no big deal.

I run across the street without looking both ways, hoping that a very large truck will slam into me. But, of course, I make it home in one piece.

Karine eyes me with repugnance. Marjorie shakes her head disapprovingly.

"*The Edge of Night* ended a long time ago. Do you know what that means?" Karine always sounds too old for her age.

"Did you see Manman before she left?" I ask them.

"Of course we saw her," Marjorie replies in a self-righteous way. "We got here when we were supposed to." She doesn't take her eyes off the silly woodpecker on TV.

"Did she ask where I was?" The woodpecker starts to laugh: *Hey-hey-hey-hey-hey!*

"We told you to come home with us," Karine says. "But you didn't listen."

The woodpecker's head shakes as it laughs: *Hey-hey-hey-hey-hey!*

"Did you tell Manman I was helping the new teacher, Mr. E?" The woodpecker is quiet now.

"Yes."

"Did she believe you?"

"No. Manman said you better hope Mr. E can save you from turning into the bouzen you're trying to become." The woodpecker starts to laugh again, a piercing sound that hurts my head.

"Did Manman call Frisner?"

"What do you think?"

I know the answer to my next question but I ask it anyway: "Is he coming?"

Both girls nod in unison. The woodpecker thinks someone is still watching the screen. *Hey-hey-hey-hey-hey!* That's the Woody Woodpecker song.

* * *

The second we hear the rattle of Frisner's keys on the other side of the door, Karine turns off the TV and grabs a textbook. She hangs her head in such a way that makes her look like she's been studying all day. Marjorie hides the mystery novel she was reading under her pillow and reaches for a science book. I open my American History book.

Frisner reaches through the hole where the knob used to be and pulls the door open violently. His fingers leave yet another layer of grease there.

"Flora."

"Oui, Papa." I follow him into the living room.

Frisner searches my eyes for a few seconds before slamming his fist into my face. I fall on the coffee table. My hands streak the glass. I'll have to clean that later.

"Bouzen!" Frisner roars. "Get up." The perfume in his clothes stings my nostrils. It's not Joie de Vivre.

He likes to hear me cry, so I don't make a sound. I squeeze my thighs together, keeping the pain from spreading.

"You think I brought you to this country to disgrace me?"

Frisner's questions are almost always rhetorical, so I don't answer. The space between his eyebrows furrows as he pulls an extension cord out of the socket, wrapping one end tightly around his fist.

The first lash falls across my shoulders and catches the right side of my face.

The second strikes lower and slides across my arm, breaking the skin. The third lash falls in the same spot as the last, freeing a small stream of blood. The urine I tried to hold burns my thighs on its way down to the parrot shit–green rug. "One day you'll thank me," Frisner says before walking away.

I move past Karine and Marjorie on the way to the kitchen for a sponge to clean up the mess. The girls don't look up from their books.

In the morning, Frisner grunts a response to our collective *Bonjour*. We slide into the backseat, leaving the passenger side empty for Manman.

When we reach the factory, Manman gets into the car so slowly you'd think every bone in her body was broken. She leans her head against the window and falls asleep. The silence inside the car is spiteful. Occasionally, Frisner shoots me a loaded look through the rearview mirror.

We reach the school after what feels like a hundred years. My sisters and I hurry out of the car as soon as it comes to a stop. When the guard gives her signal, we leap away from the Ford LTD.

"Flora!" Frisner yells in that tone policemen use when they draw their weapons and order a perpetrator to freeze.

Manman's eyes flick open, but she shuts them again quickly.

"Oui."

Frisner juts the left side of his face out the open window. He wants his daily *au revoir* kiss. I contemplate running away like those Maroons in my old *Histoire d'Haïti* textbook, but there are no mountains to hide out in around the school building.

I could defy Frisner and walk away. The crossing guards would impale him if he tried to hurt me. But would they follow me home at the end of the day to stop him from shipping me back to the island?

"You want me to get out of this car and make you kiss me?" Another rhetorical question. I pucker up and yield.

I rush to the bathroom to unravel the Flora-from-Haiti cornrows. I am late for Mrs. Williams's class, but I won't walk around school looking like I just swam to shore after my boat capsized.

I sit in the back of the classroom. Mrs. Williams lectures about the Manifest Destiny thing. I don't understand a word of it. When the bell rings, she orders me to stay behind. I watch the other students leave.

She inspects my face. Her roving eyes have tears in them. "What happened to you?"

"Nothing." What did she think I'd say?

"Did someone hurt you?"

"No."

She searches my eyes but I'm not selling any clues today. "Your grades are improving." She gives me a motherly smile. "I can tell you've been studying."

I keep my eyes on the floor, waiting for her to get through whatever her mission is. My blood is boiling. I scream inside my head, but no words leave my mouth.

"Keep up the good work." Mrs. Williams pats me on the back.

My sisters and I reach home just before *The Edge of Night* starts. Manman looks at my face and nods her appreciation. "Looks like your papa taught you a good lesson. Do yourself a favor and memorize it."

When *The Edge of Night* ends, Manman leaves for the factory. The minute the door closes behind her, Marjorie turns on the TV to watch *Batman*, *Spider-Man*, and every other mutant in a pair of flashy tights that can save the world in thirty minutes minus the commercials.

Karine is reading. But gone are her mystery novels. She graduated to a book in which women describe, in great detail, their sexual fantasies. Karine thinks no one knows about her little book. The apartment is so small that secrets are impossible to keep for too long. When Frisner finds her little book, he'll send all three of our bodies back to Haiti in a very small box.

When we hear his keys on the other side of the door, Marjorie turns off the TV and grabs a textbook. Karine hides her sexual fantasies inside her pillowcase and grunts her annoyance. I sit on my bed with the history textbook splayed open on my lap. I'm reading the English words but inside my head I am standing before Sister Bernadêtte, trying to finish my recitation. Yseult is at her desk behind me. I feel her eyes on me—they are so heavy with tears that mine well up too.

"*Toussaint Louverture voulait la guerre. La moindre occasion suffisait donc pour le provoquer. Toussaint Louverture wanted war.*" The words begin to slip away from me, slithering like zandolits, sliding toward the thorny bushes. "*Toussaint Louverture voulait la guerre . . . Toussaint Louverture wanted war.*" The lesson is gone, gone under the bushes. The words play hide and seek under the thorny bushes inside my head. "*La moindre occasion suffisait . . .*" Tears roll out of Yseult's eyes. I don't need to see her face to know how she feels. The tears on her cheeks are cold and taste like sea salt.

Sister Bernadêtte purses her lips. She juts her chin forward, tacitly directing me to start again.

I go over the first line in my head, hoping to trigger more of the lesson, but the ribbon tied to this balloon drifts too far into the sky for my arms to reach. The lesson I'd spent hours memorizing is now lost among the dense black clouds in my head. The nun is vexed. "None of the other girls forgot their lessons," she says. "Even your burnt-potato buddy, Yseult Joseph, received a perfect grade for her recitation. Flora Desormeau, what exactly is wrong with your brain? Something is wrong with your brain. I want to know what it is."

"*Toussaint Louverture voulait la guerre*," I begin again, determined to prove that nothing is wrong with my brain. "*Toussaint Louverture wanted . . .*" What did Toussaint want? There's a hiss in my head like air seeping out of a balloon.

"Useless!" Sister Bernadête shrieks, but it's Frisner I hear.

"Bonsoir, Papa," Karine and Marjorie chorus as if they'd rehearsed those words all day. He raises the brown shopping bag in his hand in acknowledgment of their greeting. I throw in as good a "Bonsoir, Papa" as I can manage.

"Flora," he says all sweet and kind, but his eyes have a raging storm in them. He gives me the brown shopping bag. His tone is a lot colder now: "Open it."

Inside the bag is a vinyl record album. Half of me thinks it's a gift; the other half knows better. The women on the cover wear shiny thigh-high boots like those ladies on the other side of the Lincoln Tunnel who beckon strangers with their index fingers and promise to thrill them to death in the backseat of cars. Their eyes sparkle like the neon lights in Times Square.

"I found this album behind the bushes," Frisner explains. "You were waiting for the right time to sneak it in here, weren't you?"

"It's not mine," I say.

"Tell the truth." He coils the extension cord around his wrist.

"It's not mine."

"Marjorie! Karine!" Frisner throws the album at them and waits for an explanation.

Marjorie looks at the cover then passes it to Karine. They shake their heads. They've never seen the album before either.

"You're all going back to Haiti tomorrow." Frisner indicates the three passports on the coffee table. "I didn't bring you to America to drift like stray cats in the street."

Marjorie lets out a scream and starts to shake her head like there's something inside she wants to get out. Frisner pinches her mouth shut. "Fèmen djòl ou. You want the neighbors to hear?"

Karine's nostrils flare. She presses her fingers against her temples. She makes a fist. "Send me back," she says. "I don't want to live near you anymore anyway."

"You'd like that, wouldn't you?" The extension cord comes down on her back with a vengeance. Lashes fall like raindrops in a hurricane.

When Frisner dismisses us, Karine and Marjorie run to their bed, burying their heads under the blanket. I slide the album under my own bed—between the box spring and the mattress. One day I'll play the record until I learn every song by heart and I will sing them loud enough for Frisner to hear.

* * *

The next morning in Mrs. Williams's class, the secretary's voice comes over the intercom. "*The following students must report to the principal's office immediately: Karine, Marjorie, and Flora Dee-zor-mo.*"

Mrs. Williams nods in my direction. She seems pleased that I am being summoned away from her classroom.

When I reach the principal's office, I find Marjorie and Karine already sitting there, hands folded in their laps like the well-mannered young ladies Manman is trying to raise. A skinny woman in a dark-brown suit gets up from her chair and introduces herself as Ms. Miller.

"Girls," the principal starts. This one is tall with a towering bouffant and a pair of reading glasses dangling from the silver chain around her neck. "I've asked you here because it's been brought to my attention that perhaps you are being physically abused. I want you to know that if this is the case, the school is prepared to take the appropriate measures to ensure that you are removed from—" She stops abruptly, searching the ceiling for just the right words. "From . . . this . . . unacceptable situation and placed in a safe environment."

She examines the bruises around my eyes. "How did you get those?" She doesn't wait for an answer. "Who did this to you?"

"I fell down." I say this quickly because I can tell she's one of those all-heart types on the hunt for her next cause. "I was running. I tripped. I broke the fall with my face. On the railroad tracks!" I regret throwing in the last detail as soon as it comes out. The incredulous look Ms. Miller exchanges with the principal tells me she'd expected me to say something like that.

"The nurse is waiting for you in her office." The principal nods continuously as she talks. Her head springs up and down like that woodpecker on TV. "I've asked her to take a look at you, if that's okay."

It's not okay with me, but Ms. Miller, Karine, and Marjorie are already halfway down the corridor. So I follow them.

The nurse sighs at the constellation of bruises on my back. "What happened?"

"Frisner happened," Karine pipes up, displaying her own collection of fresh welts and old scars.

"Who's Frisner?"

"Our papa," says Marjorie.

"He won't be able to do this to you anymore," the nurse declares. Perhaps she's planning to cut Frisner up into little pieces the minute school lets out.

There's a knock on our apartment door. "Is this the Desormeau household?"

Manman turns the TV volume down. "Yes," she says apologetically.

"My name is Ms. Miller."

Karine's hands fly to her mouth. Marjorie eyes the closet door as if she wants to hide inside. There's a sudden dampness in my hands. Manman opens the door reluctantly. She eyes the stranger with suspicion. "She's from our school," Karine explains in Creole.

Ms. Miller produces an official-looking badge with her picture on it. Manman steps aside, letting Ms. Miller in. They sit at the kitchen table. Manman fidgets, twisting her wedding band for reinforcement. "Your children have an unusual number of bruises on their bodies. Do you know who's responsible?"

Manman flashes Ms. Miller a hateful look then turns her eyes on me. She keeps them there like loaded guns.

"Does your husband beat these children?" Ms. Miller sweeps her arm at us as though we're the secret prizes behind some door in *Let's Make a Deal*.

Manman searches my face, tears brimming in her eyes. "No understand," she tells Ms. Miller in a meek voice. "No speekeen Englitch."

"The lady asks if Frisner beats us," Marjorie eagerly translates.

Ms. Miller clears her throat. Disappointment is spelled out in capital letters across her face. Her visit is futile if Manman doesn't understand a word.

Manman avoids looking directly at the woman. She keeps her eyes on us, speaking only in Creole now, each word a sharp prong in the verbal fence that keeps the stranger from trespassing.

"Ti moun," Manman says in a painful voice. "You bring this American lady here to wash her hands in my face?"

"Papa never beats us," I lie to Ms. Miller.

"We just fall down a lot," Karine agrees.

Ms. Miller shakes her head. "I cannot help you girls unless you tell me the truth."

My sisters and I glance at one another, wondering how Ms. Miller will help us once Frisner finds out about her visit.

Manman escorts her to the door and deadbolts it behind her. "I hate this country," she says through clenched teeth.

Karine and Marjorie exchange a triumphant look.

"In my country," Manman adds, "your Ms. Miller would have beaten you for betraying your papa and me."

"We're not in your country now." Karine sounds like some Joan of Arc—all armored up. Fists cocked on her hips, standing like she has an army behind her.

"And we're never going back." Marjorie sounds like one of those cartoon heroes on TV.

It's time for *The Edge of Night* to start, but Manman is not interested in soap operas today. She telephones her boss at the factory: "No feeling good today. No come to work today." Manman always asks one of us to speak English for her. Not today. Today she becomes American too.

She slams the receiver down and goes back to the kitchen table. She sits there with a catatonic look in her eyes. She rings her fingers while mumbling to herself. Occasionally, she cries out a few curses in Creole. "May the Virgin gouge out my eyes! Vyèj pete zye m! Thunder, strike me down!"

The second Frisner walks through the door, Manman tells him about Ms. Miller's visit.

"Flora betrayed us," Manman says. "Mwen pral endispoze. Pack her bags. That ingrate is going back. Get her passport. Call the airlines. Buy a one-way ticket."

Frisner takes the seat opposite Manman. He gives her one of those looks people normally exchange at funerals. He stares at the wall, the ceiling. He rings his hands. The girls and I take turns peering through the hole in the door where the knob used to be.

"He looks like a child," Karine whispers.

Frisner says something through clenched teeth. He

makes a fist but resists the urge to slam it on the table. Manman talks about grasshoppers and giants. Frisner pretends to listen.

Marjorie turns on the TV to watch Batman defeat the Joker. Karine picks up her science book and starts to read. I close my eyes and dream about finding Yseult Joseph.

PROOF

The make-believe world behind the TV screen was even more disorderly than when we first arrived in the United States, but Manman still preferred it to real life. She checked out every morning and stayed gone until it was time to leave for the factory. She traveled to faraway places, chatted with famous faces, wore fine jewelry and pretty dresses—all vicariously through the characters in the soap operas. She was such a devoted fan that tears studded her eyes when they cancelled *The Edge of Night*. She mourned as if every cast member had been a dear friend who died unexpectedly. "Yo fini avèk Raven," Manman lamented. "They got rid of Raven," one of the lead characters on the show. And if that wasn't enough, Luke and Laura had split up and remarried too many other people to count. If that marriage could dissolve like an ice cube in the noonday sun, Manman said, nothing in America was safe.

Papa kept himself busy by wrapping extension cords around his wrists and lashing me down for reasons only he understood.

Three days after my high school graduation, I stuffed a few clothes in a backpack and left. I told Karine and Marjorie I would keep in touch. But I knew I'd never return.

Mr. E, my old teacher, had given me his phone number and said I should call if ever I was in trouble. Not having a place to sleep meant that I was in trouble. So I called him.

"You can't stay at my house," he explained. "Neighbors might jump to too many ridiculous conclusions."

I was relieved when he added that he kept a small apartment in the city. He said I could stay there for as long as I needed.

"You're your own woman now," Mr. E announced on our way to his apartment in the city.

I had never thought of myself as a woman before, but I knew he was right. I belonged to myself now. Time had beaten Papa, usurped his power.

"You have quite a journey ahead of you," Mr. E prophesied. I did not answer. What was there to say?

When we reached the city, Mr. E parked in an underground lot and began to march ahead at such a rapid pace that I had to run to keep up with him.

Above ground, there was nothing to remind me of the town I'd left less than an hour earlier. The little houses and green lawns that blended into one another had vanished. Everything was concrete, steel, and colossal. Impossibly tall buildings accented with impossibly long metal fingers reached upward, tickling the sun.

Cars sped like comets. People, in various degrees of indifference, negotiated the streets—oblivious to all that was going on around them. They were unconscious beings moving through space. They drifted past without noticing us.

Mr. E and I were two nameless faces in a sea of others. We were anonymous. Invisible.

"Here we are," Mr. E said when we reached the soot-covered fire escapes decorating his building's façade. There was a brownish mirror in the ceiling of the elevator with specks of silver dotting it. The bald spot in the middle of Mr. E's head was magnified.

"Home away from home," Mr. E said when he opened the front door to his place.

A musty smell got up from the rug and slapped me in the face.

"Sorry about the mess." Mr. E flicked on a lamp. "I was not expecting company."

I wasn't sure if he was talking to me or the battalion of roaches now scurrying every which way. Some of them rushed toward the ceiling from which a chunk of plaster dangled as though it were a light fixture. On the other side of the sofa was a wooden coffee table. An empty can of Hormel chili with a plastic spoon in it sat on a hotplate with the cord wrapped around it. There was a small refrigerator on the opposite side of the room. A mildew-green vase held the remains of three roses, some ferns, and liatrice.

To the right of the refrigerator was a narrow doorway through which I could see a toilet with a shower wedged up against it. This was not a place where I would want to stay very long. A week, two, a month at most, but no more than that. I would need money. A lot of it. Fast.

"Relax," Mr. E said. "You look a little sad."

"I'm not."

He came closer and took the backpack from my shoulder. "Let's go out. This is New York, babe. Happiness is a thing you can buy from street vendors!" He turned his head in a way that reminded me of our old landlord back in Haiti.

Mr. E led us out of the apartment. The hallway was quiet, as if no one lived behind the steel doors on either side of it. Two people entered the building as we exited. Jet-black hair jutted out from their scalps. Their leather jackets were adorned with chains, metal studs, and spikes. They both wore heavy black makeup around their eyes and on their lips. There were rings on their noses, rings pierced through their eyebrows. Perhaps they were both boys, perhaps girls. I could not tell. They mumbled something to Mr. E. He waved them away and kept walking. "Old perv," they shouted behind us. Mr. E did not turn around. His pace quickened, like a thief trying to escape unnoticed and discreetly. For a moment, I wondered what they meant; then decided it was safer to keep my mind on the unknown future charging like a bull toward me.

Half a block down, I noticed a street vendor sitting before a table of children's toys. There were fire trucks, machine guns, soldiers, and robots. On a high chair next to the vendor was a doll with eyes that made her look like a real baby. She had a heart-shaped mouth and long black curls that glistened in the streetlights. She wore a lace-trimmed bib—just like the doll that had disappeared from the upstairs bedroom in Haiti.

KARINE AND MARJORIE

The girls meet every Saturday afternoon for espresso and biscotti at a café on Mulberry Street. Karine is now a second-year law student at NYU; Marjorie is almost done with her studies at the College of Dentistry. Their weekly ritual on Mulberry Street began years ago when the two were shopping for knock-off designer purses on Canal Street. They had parked their car at the corner of Broadway and Prince. The location is important because that's precisely the spot where they saw Flora—or a girl who looked just like their sister. They followed her through the throngs buzzing about the stalls heaped with faux Mont Blanc pens, Rolex watches, and Dior sunglasses. The girl turned left on Mulberry and went into the café. Karine and Marjorie waited outside for her. They waited for a while and then ventured inside to inquire about the girl. "Are you sure she came in here?" the waiter asked. "No one fitting your description came in here." Karine and Marjorie wondered why the man would lie about such a thing. They had seen Flora; they were both certain of it. They went back to the street, looking every which way. "There!" Karine said when she saw the girl come out of another restaurant. They chased her, calling out, "Flora! Flora!" But the girl did not turn around. Marjorie, unfaltering as those cartoon superheroes she used to love, caught the girl by the arm. "I'm sorry," she said, "I thought you were someone else."

They return to the café on Mulberry every Saturday, sitting always by the window—hoping that Flora might happen by. She never does.

Today Marjorie brings along a newspaper clipping she knows her sister will find interesting. The headline's bold letters leap off the page: *Shocking Breach of Trust!*

Karine's hand flies to her mouth when she reads the article: *Retired school teacher is convicted of luring unsuspecting immigrant students into* . . . The teacher, flanked by police officers, has a jacket covering his face, but Karine recognizes him right away. She shakes her head in disbelief. "How can that man work in the school system for so long and not get caught?"

Marjorie hunches her shoulders. "People like to pretend men like him don't exist. So they ignore the glaring signs. I refuse to believe his colleagues didn't know."

"Sure they knew. I guess it was easier to look the other way. As long as it wasn't happening to their own children, right?"

"Right. But he's just one of who knows how many, prancing in classrooms all over the world, waiting. And it's not just men. They've caught women doing the same. They prey on little kids all day long, scare them to death while they destroy their lives."

"Thank God they took this jerk out of commission."

"To think he was our teacher!" The past envelops both girls in its vast wings, silencing them for the moment.

The paper says that a children's advocate from Brazil, Fatima C., was instrumental in helping the state win its case against Mr. E.

PART III
Yseult

YSEULT JOSEPH

In the morning when the maid walks me to school, I make her stop by my best friend's house. I take Flora's hand as soon as I see her. We giggle and run the rest of the way.

The maid trails behind like an old lady on wobbly legs, but she doesn't miss much with her bulging eyes. She tells me to slow down and watch out for passing cars. I tell her: "Yvela, I give the orders. Not you." That usually shuts her up.

Once Flora and I reach the other side of the school's iron gate, Yvela retraces her steps and goes back home, like a good dog.

At the sound of the first bell, Flora and I line up in the courtyard with Sister Bernadête's sixth grade class. There are eight rows, one for each grade level; twenty-five girls in each.

The students wear white shirts and pleated black skirts that fall below our knees. The nuns wear floor-length habits and immaculate white guimpes that cover their chests, shoulders, and necks. The wide bandeau under Sister Bernadête's veil conceals her hair (which I suspect is yellow and wispy like chicken feathers). The silver crucifix accentuates the pale blue of her eyes.

Everyone faces the towering flagpole. We will not be able to read the caption once the flag is raised: *L'Union fait La Force* (Unity Is Strength), but we will trust that no one tampered with it overnight; that it is still there.

Flora and I throw our voices high to declare our love for our country and flag.

Afterward, we follow Sister Bernadête to the classroom one story above the courtyard.

Sister Bernadête has separated us on numerous occasions, but somehow Flora and I always end up sitting side by side, like the wings of a hummingbird. We share textbooks. We read at the same pace. We get stuck on the same big words. We laugh when we're supposed to be quiet, and we get in trouble for it.

Sister Bernadête shoots us viperous looks and draws her lips together. She shakes her head at us, as though we are an anomaly: Flora Desormeau and Yseult Joseph. Two bodies, one head.

When we're lucky, Sister Bernadête banishes us to the back of the classroom and orders us to spend an hour on our knees. "Face the wall!" the nun shrieks. "Don't let me see your ugly faces today!"

Flora and I welcome Sister Bernadête's punishment. We don't cry and feel sorry for ourselves. We look out the window that offers a panoramic view of what must be the greatest hotel in Haiti. Sister Bernadête thinks we're staring at the blank wall, but what would be the point of that? What a waste of time that would be.

The thatched roofs covering the cabins surrounding the hotel's main building are there only for decoration. There's nothing back-country about Cabane Choucoune. The cabins have electricity (even at night!), running water, and toilets that are not wooden boxes with holes on top—like the ones at school.

Cabane Choucoune's grounds are punctuated with majestic palm trees, bougainvilleas, hibiscus, and white roses that cover a pergola ten thousand kilometers long.

Flora and I could spend days watching the tourists splash around in a pool as wide as the Artibonite River. Sometimes they roll around in the grass, kissing and caressing one another as if life were made for nothing more.

Sometimes they have sex right in the pool—with everyone's eyes on them, but not seeing. They think the water is capable of keeping their secret. But the pool, like the hue of the Caribbean blue it tries to imitate, is deceiving.

Flora and I see everything from our punishment corner in Sister Bernadête's sky. Like two angels hovering, we see it all.

Sometimes naked tourists flap against one another like fish out of water. When they quit flapping and start to tremble, Flora and I hook our pinkies together and say the magic words: "Sa ki kole pa gen dwa dekole." We defy them to get unstuck. But our magic is powerless against tourists.

Some people think Flora and I are sisters, but we are not. They say we look alike. That is more than fine with me. Flora Desormeau is beautiful. Her skin is the color of the almond candy Manman used to make before Papa went away.

Manman doesn't spend much time in the kitchen shed anymore. She leaves the cooking to Yvela.

Manman used to put good things in my lunchbox

before Papa left too: ham sandwiches, raisins, mango slices. Now Manman tells me to eat whatever the nuns serve in the canteen: cornmeal mush, watered-down milk, and more cornmeal mush.

After lunch in the canteen, Flora and I spend the recreation period playing oslè near the grotto with the statue of the Virgin Mary in it. Sometimes as we play, Flora gets that faraway look in her eyes. Her heart tightens and her stomach aches. When that happens, my heart tightens and my stomach aches too. We feel this way because both of our fathers went to live in New York. Flora cannot talk about her papa without crying. She misses him—not for herself, she says, but for her manman. She was easier to love before he took the plane and left.

Once a month Manman talks to Papa on the phone, and she asks me to say a few words before she hangs up. I ask him about Flora's father. He says he has no idea where the man is. "New York is a big place," he assures me. "People don't run into one another the way they do in small villages, on tiny islands."

When Papa sends for me and I go to New York finally, I will write Flora a letter every day. I'll let her know that I'm always thinking about her. I won't give her the chance to miss me.

When Flora's papa sends for her and she comes to New York, she will find me. We'll go to the same school. We'll sit side by side, like the wings of a hummingbird. I'll make my New York maid stop by Flora's house to pick her up every morning, just like I do here. Nothing will keep us apart.

THE PRICE OF BEAUTY

Pina was shaped like a warped goose gourd. You couldn't squeeze her bottom half into a fifty-five gallon drum, but her head, arms, and chest might slide through the eye of a needle without much effort. She walked with a limp, her back had a hump. Her eyes—well, the one that worked opened only to a squint. Despite these limitations, Pina was as strong as a breadfruit tree whose roots extended for miles underground. A category-five hurricane could not knock that woman down.

"You're mine now," Pina said one afternoon, fists cocked on her hips. She was standing in the bedroom doorway, winking her good eye at the terrified child.

Yseult knew what Pina wanted. She tried to run, but Pina blocked her way with an outstretched arm. Yseult opened her mouth and clamped down on Pina's wrist with every one of her thirty-two teeth. The salt in Pina's skin nauseated her. Still, Yseult dug her teeth in deeper, like an enraged animal.

The sudden pain stunned Pina into loosening her grip. She raised a hand to slap Yseult. In that instant, a gap opened between her hip and the doorpost. Yseult slipped through it and bolted toward the backyard. Pina kicked off her sandals and took off after her.

Manman, who had been standing just outside the door, threw her hands up and half-laughed before joining in the chase. The two of them screamed for the neighbors to catch Yseult as if she were a thief who had broken into their pantry and stolen their last grain of rice.

Yvela stepped out of the kitchen shed to watch the spectacle. "Don't let her get away!" Pina shouted. Yvela did not budge. She just stood there, still as a dumbfounded doe. She knew that Pina's sole mission in life was to torment every child who had the misfortune of being born female on the island. Yseult ran to the far end of the yard and latched on to the avocado tree, wishing that she could change colors like a chameleon and assume the leaves' variegated tone; wishing also that she could climb to the highest branch and wait there until Pina's sadistic interest waned.

"May the Virgin gouge out my eyes!" Pina swore, and spat a mouthful of curses on the ground. She was beyond annoyed at Yseult for making her run around so. Yvela was within reach, so Pina smacked her. Hard. But the girl was accustomed to being struck and Pina's blow did not faze her in the least. Realizing this, Pina tried a different strategy: she promised to send Yvela away if she refused to help. Yvela quickly joined Pina and Manman in their effort.

"Yseult Joseph, don't make me have to peel you off of there!" Manman shouted. The child clung to the tree even tighter. After all, Yseult reasoned, Manman once told her that this tree would save her life one day. Manman was so certain of it that she grafted Yseult to the avocado's roots by burying there the stump of the lifeline that had joined them in the womb.

Pina was now moving around the tree in a slow, feline fashion. "Give up, Yseult! All that defiance will only make you bleed more."

"So true," Manman shrugged her shoulders and bent over at the waist and opened her arms wide to catch Yseult in the same manner that Yvela sometimes spread her arms to catch a chicken in the yard. After an unceremonious beheading, Yvela would dip the carcass into a pot of scalding water to expedite the tedious task of plucking feathers one by one by one.

Yseult could not scream through the fear clogging her throat. But she could run. She let go of the tree, spun on her heels, and darted toward the north end of the yard. That direction funneled into the busiest intersection in town. Manman, Pina, and Yvela were now only inches away. But Yseult knew they would have to stop as soon as she reached the street. They would not risk being burdened by the memory of a speeding car cutting off Yseult's chances of seeing her next birthday.

"Let her get away," Manman shouted at Yvela, "and I'll break you like a broomstick."

A dozen braids stuck up and out in every direction from Yvela's sweat-drenched scalp. Swifter than a gazelle, she easily outran both Manman and Pina, and had Yseult by the arm in a matter of seconds.

"Damn that witch," Yvela heaved. Her breath smelled like a goat. Globs of perspiration fell over her eyes. She wiped them off with the back of her hand and pushed Yseult toward the open door of a neighbor's house, saying: "Hide!" Yvela flashed the child one of her tamarind-pod grins.

* * *

Manman and Yseult had taken Papa to the airport that morning. He looked handsome in the new white shirt that ballooned in the breeze and flapped against his skin. He wore the Panama hat that he had bought especially for the occasion.

Yseult had never seen her father so dressed up before. He held Manman for a long time before climbing the shiny metal steps that led to the airplane's narrow doorway. When he reached the top, he took off his hat, held it against his chest, and hung his head down like someone paying his last respects over a dead body.

When he lifted his head to meet the scorching sun again, he waved the hat back and forth as if he were fanning his face, but that was just his way of saying goodbye to the tropical heat. Goodbye poverty. Goodbye daughter. Goodbye wife. Goodbye Haiti.

When all the passengers had boarded the plane and the door was pulled shut, Yseult and her manman rushed to the observation room where family members of other dearly-departeds had gathered to engage in the fantasy that their loved ones were also staring back at them through the airplane's tiny windows.

The air in the observation room stood still. Everyone waved feverish goodbyes. Small children pressed their mouths against the glass, kissing and licking it as much as they pleased. The adults who might have pulled them away from the grime were too busy studying the airplane to notice.

As the plane positioned itself for the inevitable, the room became silent. Faces took on bewildered looks. Everyone seemed shocked that the plane could do more than hiss and burp and tacitly threaten to vanish behind the clouds.

Some of the left-behinds—wives, husbands, children, and assorted distant relatives—bobbed their heads like fledglings, hoping that the plane now taxiing down the runway would soon return with enough goodies in its metal bill to sate their newfound hunger. When the plane stopped abruptly, as if one of the passengers had demanded to be let out, Yseult's manman gasped. Everyone in the observation room regained their ability to speak; some even called out to the family member who was undoubtedly strapped in a seat, bracing himself for the unknown.

Yseult called out to her papa. Perhaps he would jump from the airplane and go back home with them. Perhaps the sky would open wide enough to allow the observation room with its broken-hearted congregation to ascend to New York too. Then everyone could stroll on honey-lacquered boulevards and pluck fortunes from those very special trees that were said to grow there in profusion. Perhaps . . .

Yseult's daydreaming ended abruptly when the plane's engine revved up again, announcing with a stabbing shriek that it had no intention of staying put. Some impatient passenger must have told the pilot to hurry. The plane was now speeding down the runway with the fury of a skinless midnight woman at daybreak, going faster and faster until its nose, wings, and tail were all up in the air.

Manman watched the plane as fixedly as she had looked into her husband's face before he walked past the gatekeepers who were prepared to impale anyone who even thought about slipping past them without proper documentation. She did not blink as the plane continued its sacred ascension. Her lips quivered like they did at church when she knelt before the statue of Our Lady of Perpetual Help. She was now staring at the plane in such a way that made Yseult think her mother had the power to will it back down, if she were so inclined.

Manman continued her clenched-teeth prayer, as if she feared that uttering a single word out loud would bring about considerable disruption to the natural order of things: Time would rewind like tape in a flimsy cassette; the weeks that had preceded Papa's noonday flight would be erased; every goodbye would be taken back. Every memory which had been stored as neatly and efficiently as thread in a dressmaker's bobbin would come spooling out, leaving an empty space where the indispensable had been. Nicknames no one else would recognize, birthdays, up-the-road and around-the-corner places without street names or addresses, first words, first steps, first communions, first kisses, last kisses, favorite foods: Every memory would be deleted. Purged.

Manman's prayers would snatch Papa out of the airplane and make him ride home with them. Papa would take back all the sad words he had said to kin, neighbors, and friends. He would remove his new Panama hat and the soft white shirt that billowed against his skin. He would unpack his suitcase and change into his work clothes: denim overalls and a threadbare shirt. Papa would then cover the town with his footsteps, crying out, "Men shan-y, men shan-y," and ringing the little bell that announced his presence.

"Men shan-y, men shan-y," he would wail over and

over until some kind stranger would stop him with a flick of the hand. The kind stranger would place his dusty soles on Papa's shoeshine box, light a Comme Il Faut cigarette, and blow gray smoke into Papa's face. Papa would whistle a bolero tune while he worked on the layers of dust covering the stranger's shoes.

The plane's wings shot through the clouds. Manman's prayers were powerless against the propellers, the massive engines, and the tanks of fuel that couldn't wait to thrust the mammoth bird onward and upward until it reached another world.

The sky swallowed Papa's plane whole. All everyone could do was watch. There was no reversal of events. The sun carried on with its routine revolution. Time, according to a clock on the wall, moved forward by the second. "Well, it's over," Manman said, as if she'd been watching Kanaval floats go by. And now that the last float had disappeared from view, Mardi Gras season was done. Time for everyone to rub the excitement out of her eyes and head back home.

Some of the other left-behinds in the observation room started to cry like the sort of mourners who have to be pulled away from caskets, lest they topple them with their thrashing about, and startle the dead with their screams. The other children in the observation room cried too, calling out their New York–bound relatives' names and asking questions like, *When is so-and-so coming back?* That was when Manman took Yseult's hand and rushed out of the airport as if the roof had blown off.

She didn't speak another word until the jitney dropped them off in front of their house. And then it was: "Take off that good dress, Yseult Joseph." Those words came with such a violent finger wag that Yseult knew better than to make Manman tell her twice.

Yseult ran to the bedroom and changed into her everyday clothes. She was trying to picture her papa inside the plane when that warped goose gourd, Pina, appeared in the doorway. Fists cocked on her hips, saying, "You're mine now!" Her gold upper teeth glinted behind a most malignant grin.

For years Manman had tried to convince Papa to allow Pina to perform her wicked craft on Yseult. "It's tradition," Manman had argued. "Every girl goes through it." Papa had refused: "Not my daughter." When Manman persisted, he barred Pina from the house indefinitely.

Not my daughter. Papa had been resolute in his belief that Pina's craft did nothing but cause girl children unnecessary pain. "She can have it done when she's old enough to decide for herself. Women in their fifties are having it done nowadays. Why should we allow that old witch to torture our daughter for something so trivial?"

"You're right," Manman finally agreed one Sunday after church. Pina's work was unnecessary, as Papa had always maintained. And the way in which Pina did it was barbaric. "I'll tell Pina to stay away," Manman said to Yseult. She promised to uphold Papa's decision. Even if he died.

But going to New York was worse than dying: one was unnatural, calculated; the other was not. Now that Papa had chosen to leave her, Manman saw no reason to keep her word. When they'd married, he promised to live with her forever. Not take a plane and abandon her with a child. She needed help to raise a girl child in Haiti. She needed Pina's help.

"Hide!" Yvela shouted again while shoving Yseult into the neighbor's house.

"Dog shit!" Pina roared. Yvela would pay for her actions with a severe beating. For now, Pina's sole intention was to catch Yseult and carry out what she believed was her life's calling.

Yseult ran into the house with Pina and Manman close behind. Because she was not familiar with the layout of the neighbor's house, she could not find a hiding place as quickly as she hoped. Her chances of eluding Pina were better in the wide open.

Manman tried to stop Yseult from running out, but the grief of watching Papa leave earlier must have weighed her down so much that she moved with a great degree of lethargy. Yseult got away.

Yvela had regained her dumbfounded-doe stance. She was no longer motivated to help capture Yseult; Pina could strike her and cause her to bleed, but she did not have the authority to throw her out with the trash. She was bluffing; Yvela belonged to Manman and Yseult. Not Pina. And Yvela could tell that Manman needed her now more than ever. There was no point in her doing anything but watch her boss and Pina huff and groan as they pursued Yseult, who waved as she ran back toward the house where the chase had begun.

The turtle which Manman kept in a glass bowl by the front door—to ward off evil spirits—stuck its head out and swiveled its impassive eyes.

When Yseult reached the bedroom, she slipped under the bed and tried not to breathe. The sagging mattress and the sheets smelled like the shoeshine box Papa carried around town for extra money.

"I've got you now," Manman said when she stepped into the room and plopped down on the bed. The dilapidated box spring was now inches from Yseult's face. Pina followed her in and then shut the door. They had closed the trap; Yseult knew it. But her Maroon blood would not let her surrender.

Yseult waited under the bed for something to happen, but nothing did. The room was filled with a deafening hush. Seconds dragged on forever. Pina and Manman, two women quite good at screaming in silence, signaled a plan to confuse the child by shuffling about, as if they were in the marketplace on the eve of a hurricane. Then Manman's hands appeared under the bed, pulling Yseult by the ankles—a breech birth. Pina was standing above her now, and secured both of Yseult's hands in just one of hers.

Yseult kicked and struggled while they carried her to the kitchen shed. Had she been as dumb as a sheep before its shearer, she would not have fought them at all. She would have strolled cheerfully into the shed. But because Yseult knew about the pain which Pina had the coldness of heart to inflict on girls, she wanted to kill her enemy (and Manman) before they had the chance to harm her.

Pina fenced Yseult in with her powerful thighs and proclaimed her triumph with a wicked cackle. Manman held her daughter in place by pressing down on the spot between Yseult's shoulders where she should have been born with two enormous wings.

"Here," Manman said, and Pina snatched the sharp instrument from her accomplice's hand. Pina spat on it three times—to sterilize it.

"Papa!" Yseult screamed loud enough to split the kitchen walls, but of course those walls had seen too many chickens die to either split or care.

"You hear that?" Pina whispered.

"What?" Manman replied.

Pina raised a finger toward the roof. "A plane just landed."

"Yes," Manman said. "I hear it too. Papa came back to save his precious girl."

Both women laughed.

Pina cupped her fingers under Yseult's chin and swiveled her head from side to side. She narrowed her good eye as if a bright laser beam would shoot through it to pinpoint the exact spot where she would start her work. She released Yseult's chin and, with a swift move, took hold of the left earlobe. She rubbed the skin in rapid movements, as if she were trying to spark a fire. After a few seconds of this, Pina flicked her wrist back, driving the needle through.

"Papa!" Yseult yelped.

"I told you his plane just landed on the roof," Pina barked.

"Your papa will save you," Manman growled, and then laughed a laugh so strange it sounded like someone crying.

Pina chewed the inside of her mouth mechanically as she worked the needle in and out. She shifted her weight on the bench before taking the other earlobe between her thumb and forefinger. Her good eye focused on Yseult's face with the intensity of a sculptor contemplating a stone.

When she had located the exact spot to create a matching earring of blood and thread, Pina forced the needle through the skin. But all the rubbing and pinching produced no anesthetizing effect.

Each time the needle pierced Yseult's skin, something like a glass globe exploded inside her head. Jagged pieces scattered and stabbed the soft places behind the girl's eyes, blinding her.

Pina was oblivious to Yseult's pain. She continued to chew the inside of her mouth mechanically as she worked. When she was through, she heaved a sigh of satisfaction; she had completed her mission.

Manman released her hold of Yseult's shoulders and walked around to face her. "Still ugly," she said and spat on the floor. "Girls are supposed to look pretty when they get their ears pierced, but you're uglier now than before."

"Girls have to suffer to be beautiful." Pina slapped her thigh as she laughed.

"Maybe she didn't suffer enough."

"Well," Manman said, "the sooner she starts suffering, the better off she'll be." She looked at Yseult as she talked, but if it had been dark and you couldn't see her face, you would have sworn Manman was talking to herself.

THE MULÂTRESSE
AND THE MEN ON THE MOON

Papa sent another cassette from New York. Manman tripped and fell on the way to popping it into our cassette player. His voice rose from the small speaker like steam from a tureen of pumpkin soup on New Year's Day.

"*How is my femme?*" He paused for a few seconds, waiting for her to begin her part of the make-believe dialogue.

Manman whispered, "One day good, one day bad." Her face quivered. She hunched her shoulders to express the feelings for which words did not exist.

Papa's tone wasn't as soft when he asked about me. He did not pause for me to answer. It was still difficult, he said, to send for us. "*It takes money I do not have. You understand, don't you, sweetheart?*" Manman nodded. Papa filled the rest of the cassette with American music, slow songs full of sad notes and words which Manman and I did not understand.

Manman listened to that cassette every night. Since we slept in the same bed, Papa's voice and the sad songs took root inside my head. "*Ay bee dère, before the next teardrop falls . . .*" I could not stop singing on the way to school.

Yvela soon learned the lyrics from me and we both

couldn't stop cooing, "*Ay bee dère*." When I reached home from school in the afternoon, Yvela and I continued to sing around the house. Manman threatened to cut out both our tongues if we didn't stop, so we did.

Yvela's sad eyes belonged in an old woman's face. When her mother left her with us, she told Manman: "Keep her as long as you want. I have more girl children than I can use at home."

Manman sent Yvela to night school one day a week, keeping the promise she had made to Yvela's mother— even though we never saw that woman again.

Yvela's classmates were other rèstavèks and peasants who wanted to be able to write their names at least once before they died. Night school didn't teach Latin, cate-chism, or embroidery—that suited Yvela just fine. Sister Bernadêtte would have despised her anyway. Yvela did not know how to speak a word of French. And she was not interested in learning how to dislocate her jaw at will, to say things like, *Je jure devant Dieu et devant la nation. I swear before God and before the nation* . . .

Yvela practiced writing her name on every scrap of paper she could find. She wrote her name in the mar-gins of her *Ti Malice* textbook. She wrote her name on the kitchen wall with a piece of charcoal, but Manman made her wash it off.

Using the handle of a wooden spoon, Yvela created a circle of letters in the dirt around the little chair she sat on to cook our meals. The letters spelled out her name nine times.

When I was not in school, Yvela and I sat on the rooftop to admire the mulâtresse's beautiful house next door. A bed of rags protected our skin from the scorching tin. The branches from the mulâtresse's fruit trees spread out over our heads, some low enough to touch. Yvela and I feasted on clusters of kenèp and ripe mangoes until our stomachs hurt. When the sun went down, we sat on the front porch where Yvela gladly recounted the stories her grandmother taught her before she came to live with Manman and me.

When Yvela ran out of stories to tell, we counted the stars in the sky and searched the moon for the men Manman said the Americans had sent there.

One afternoon when Yvela and I were on the rooftop, we saw the mulâtresse sitting in front of her coiffeuse, brushing the longest black hair I had ever seen.

"She reminds me of La Sirène," Yvela said in a dreamy voice.

"What's that?" I wanted to know.

"Not *what*. Who," Yvela replied. "La Sirène is the queen of the sea. She's so beautiful anyone who sees her face would rather go blind than look away."

"Maybe they're twins," I said. "The mulâtresse and La Sirène."

"They're not." Yvela shuddered with disgust at my ignorance. "The queen of the sea's skin is the color of a new penny. The mulâtresse is yellow like okra blossoms."

Yvela closed her eyes and talked about the queen of the sea as if she could see her: "La Sirène sits on a float in the middle of the ocean. Her float is decorated with pretty tinsels and sequins that sparkle in the sun. If you want a closer look, you have to take a boat. If you wait for her to come to the shore, you might wait forever."

"Is La Sirène's hair long like the mulâtresse's?" I asked.

"La Sirène's hair is longer," said Yvela. "Her hairbrush is real gold and studded with precious stones."

"If I ever see that brush, I'll steal it for Manman. She could brush her hair every day until it grows as long and pretty as the mulâtresse's. Papa would have to come back from New York to stare at Manman forever."

"No one can steal La Sirène's hairbrush," Yvela fired back. "Those who try always drown. Their families never hear from them again. But if you're nice and if La Sirène likes you, she'll give you one, especially if you don't ask. Once you have the brush, you become a magnet for all the riches in the world."

"La Sirène must have given her jeweled hairbrush to the mulâtresse," I said. "She's the richest woman in all of Haiti."

"Maybe," Yvela replied. "Or maybe the mulâtresse sold her soul for her riches." Yvela then plucked a cluster of kenèp from a branch above her head. She broke the rind with her teeth and sucked the fleshy seeds ravenously. She swallowed the juice in a loud gulp and let the crumbs rain on the rooftop.

"The mulâtresse's house is bigger than the National Palace," I said. "Bigger than that great cathedral in Port-au-Prince that Manman goes to on special occasions."

"La Sirène's house is bigger than the National Palace and the cathedral put together." Yvela was more than a little annoyed at my lack of knowledge. "La Sirène's house takes up the entire bottom of the sea." She fixed her eyes on the mountains in the distance. The four o'clock sun beamed down on her black face. Little bubbles of sweat dotted her broad nose. Her hair smelled like coconut oil. I kept my eyes on the mulâtresse's yard. Uncle Lazarre, the gardener, was busy pruning roses and shaping bougainvillea hedges as usual. The mulâtresse's new car looked like a hearse. The chauffeur, perpetually dressed in a dark suit and hat, looked like an undertaker. He spat on a rag and polished the little metal wings of the lady perched on the hood of the mulâtresse's car. The silver bullets in the security guard's bandolier gave off sparks. He cradled the rifle in his arms as though it were a newborn baby. Several maids in crisp uniforms ran in and out of the house. Some carried enormous bouquets of flowers; others had brooms and dust rags.

"Let's go," Yvela eventually said. It was time for her to cook our dinner. I didn't like to stay on the roof by myself, so I followed her. She went to the kitchen shed and made plantain mush with anise stars, milk, cinnamon, and sugar. She served Manman her bowl of labouyi bannan in bed, as usual. Since Papa went to New York, Manman spent a lot of time sleeping. When she was not baking gato for people, Manman slept—often with a very dissatisfied look on her face.

Yvela and I took our dinner on the front porch. Afterward, she told me about a lady who roamed the midnight streets in search of a child she'd lost a hundred years before Yvela's own great-grandmother was even born. "Can't you hear her weeping?" Yvela asked.

Sometimes when the streets were quiet, I could hear the woman weep, but now it was the shrill siren of an ambulance that was stabbing my ears. The noise died in the mulâtresse's driveway.

Yvela said we had to go inside right away. "A bad spirit will soon pass by." She tried to pull me into the house, but I pushed her away. I wanted to know what was going on in the mulâtresse's yard. "Let's go to the roof and look," I suggested.

Yvela scrunched up her face. "People will see us up there and think we're skinless midnight women."

"There is no such thing," I said. Sister Bernadête told us that parents invented the skinless women lougarous to scare bad children. The nun said that no woman had the ability to peel off her skin and grow wings at night. "What woman would want to, even if she could?" Sister Bernadête said. "Women should be so busy during the day that all they want to do at night is sleep."

"Then go up by yourself," Yvela countered, knowing that I would not. "We have to get into the house right away," she pleaded.

I shook my head. "You're my rèstavèk. You should do as I say."

"The bad spirit will eat you," Yvela responded, grabbing my arm and dragging me into the house. She locked the front door and then put the broomstick behind it—to keep the bad spirit away.

"I don't believe in your bad spirits," I mumbled.

"You want me to call Danmadjou for you?" Yvela asked. "He'll make you believe."

"Who's Danmadjou?"

"Danmadjou was a charcoal vendor in the province where I come from. I used to buy from him all the time—until he fell into a ravine along with his mule and broke his neck. When he returned months later, his arms and legs had grown so long that they dragged on the street as he rode up and down. People hired him to fix little children who disobeyed their grown-ups. All I have to do is say his name three times and he'll be here. You want me to call him?"

"Go on and call him," I said. "I'll spit in his face."

"Danmadjou," Yvela whispered. "Danmadjou." She searched my face for signs of fear. She started to call out the charcoal vendor's name a third time, so I pressed my hand on her mouth, stopping her—just in case.

"Okay," I said. "I'll go to bed."

Yvela flashed a victorious grin.

"At least I don't sleep under a table like a dog!" I enjoyed watching her grin disappear.

Manman was snoring. The bowl of labouyi bannan was still on the table by her side of the bed. She'd barely touched it. Since Papa went to New York, she ate very little. "I've lost my appetite," she would say, as if appetite were a lucky charm she had pinned to the inside of her dress and it had fallen off without her noticing.

The American music from Papa's cassette filled the room. I could say the words much better now: "*I'll be there before the next teardrop falls.*" When I reached over to turn off the tape, Manman jerked awake suddenly and started the cassette from the beginning where Papa asked, "*How is my femme?*"

When the cassette ended, I pressed my head against the pillow and fell asleep.

Inside a dream I saw a large car in front of our house. I peered into it—naturally. The mulâtresse was in the backseat with her hands folded demurely in her lap. A black mantilla shielded her face. She told me to get in. I didn't want to, but I did. The door closed and the chauffeur revved up the engine. We drove for miles but went only as far as her house next door. The chauffeur came around and opened the back door. The mulâtresse pushed me out. She said she didn't like me always looking at her house. I ran away from the car and hid behind the bougainvilleas. I glanced up and saw Papa on the rooftop. I called out to him, but my voice could not reach him. When the mulâtresse found me crouched behind the bougainvilleas, she laughed a vicious laugh and said that since I liked to peep through her windows so much, maybe I wanted to come into the house for a closer look. When she pushed me through her front door, I screamed myself awake.

I inched closer to Manman's side of the bed. I wanted to tell her about my dream, but dared not wake her. I wanted to tell Yvela, but I was terrified of taking a step in the dark. I squeezed my eyes shut and prayed for daylight.

When morning finally came, I told Yvela about my dream. She said that if Papa hadn't gone to New York, no one would have been able to take me away. Not even in a dream.

I avoided the roof for a while, but then one day Yvela said she wanted to eat some mangoes, so I followed her up there. I didn't want to peep into the mulâtresse's yard or window ever again, but what else could I do?

Down in the yard, I saw two of the mulâtresse's maids standing together, talking. Uncle Lazarre, as usual, was tending to the roses and bougainvilleas. The maids' voices wafted up to the rooftop: "Madame put on her most expensive gown. She loaded her neck and fingers with jewelry. She wore enough perfume to make a dead rat smell pretty."

"I fixed her the cup of tea she asked for," said the other maid. "She never liked to sit outside at night, but she told me to bring her tea to the patio, so I did." The maid sounded a little sad. "Madame finished her tea. Put the cup on the table next to her. Patted down the wrinkles on her gown. Folded her hands on her lap. Closed her eyes. And died. Isn't that strange?"

Yvela and I both gasped.

"Nothing strange about it," the first maid replied. "Some people know when it's their time."

"But with Madame gone, how are we supposed to get paid? What are we supposed to do for money?"

"Beg?" the first maid offered. She sucked her teeth and spat hard on a dazzling flower bed.

"What about the house? Is it going to sit here with all those expensive things inside?"

"I heard that Madame left everything to Lazarre. House, furniture, roses, china, jewelry, perfume. All of it goes to the old gardener."

"What?"

"Madame didn't have a husband, no children. She left her house to her servant; that's what she wanted."

"Let's go," Yvela whispered in my ear.

"Quit telling me what to do."

Yvela's fingers ripped through a cluster of kenèp like a rake. The fruit scattered on the tin roof, alerting the maids to our presence.

"Get down from there, you black bats." One of the maids scooped up a handful of dirt and hurled it at us.

"San fanmi! Motherless children!" they shrieked.

"Servants!" Yvela yelled back contemptuously.

"Rèstavèk!" both maids chorused. The insult stung

so hard that Yvela's face twitched. "Maids get paid," one of them added. "Maids don't sleep in kitchen sheds or under tables like dogs."

Yvela said nothing. We made our way down from the rooftop as the maids continued to spew more insults. She fixed supper and served Manman her bowl of rice pudding in the bedroom. Afterward, Yvela and I took our dinner on the front porch. As we ate, I asked her to tell me one of her stories.

"I don't know any stories," she lied.

We sat quietly in the darkness. I counted the stars in the sky and searched the moon. As usual, I lost count of the stars and never saw the men up there.

When it was time for bed, Yvela closed the front door and put the broomstick behind it. I went to the bedroom and put my head down on the pillow next to Manman. Papa's sad songs flooded the room like rainwater after a hurricane. I pronounced the lyrics as well as the singer now, but still did not know what they meant: "*I'll be there before the next teardrop falls.*"

Once again I dreamed about the mulâtresse. Her car stopped at the front porch and I got in. We drove to her house. She scolded me for peeping through her window and then tried to push me into her house. Papa was on the rooftop again. I called out to him, but he could not hear me. I awoke and waited anxiously for the sun to get up from its bed. I would tell Yvela about my dream. She would say something wise to make me feel better.

When morning came, I found Manman in the kitchen shed, frying a couple of eggs and scraping the black off two slices of bread.

"Where's Yvela?" I asked

"Gone."

"Where did she go?"

"Who knows?" Manman was annoyed. "She probably took one of those boats that never quite make it to their destination. Everybody wants to leave this country these days. She's probably halfway to New York by now." She sighed heavily. "Your papa claims it's beautiful over there. Then again, maybe your little Yvela is at the bottom of the sea. I hear it's beautiful there too."

"Who will take me to school? Cook our food? Take me to Flora's house? Who will sit with me on the rooftop? Who will help me look for the men the Americans sent to the moon?"

"I'll talk to Ma Tante Anna," Manman said in a barely audible voice. "I'll see if she can keep you for me for a little while. It won't be long before we leave the island ourselves."

OUR LADY OF HIGH GRACE

It didn't bother Enide that she would miss her only child's wedding. She'd pleaded with Patrick not to go through with it; twenty was far too young to make such an important decision. So what if the girl would be eight months pregnant when she teetered down the aisle? Wasn't she the one who had spread her legs? Why should her son have to pay? Children were born every day without a man around to call Papa, Enide had argued. Patrick refused to hear a word. Enide begged and begged her son to abandon the marriage idea. He said he was his own man; he would do as he pleased. Exasperated, Enide had thrown her hands up and told him to sleep well in the pak koshon pigsty he'd made of his future.

At forty-six (and looking at least a decade younger), Enide had plenty of living to do. She was not about to sit around crying for Patrick. The impoverished island could not take her where she wanted to go (and there were so many places she wanted to see), so she left everything and everyone in it, including her beloved son.

Brooklyn drew Enide's strong-coffee looks into itself (black was beautiful then). The city offered to take her anywhere, give her anything she wanted—within reason, of course. She picked night school and husband number three: Luis Rivera, a widower who loved her more than he believed it possible to love anyone—in spite of all the friends and family members who shunned him for not despising Haitians like "all good Dominicans should," as one of his friends had said.

Luis presented his bride with the gold Our Lady of High Grace pendant that had belonged to his deceased mother. Enide promised to cherish it.

Within a few years, Enide had picked up enough English to complete a nurse's aid program. The school's placement service dispatched her to a sprawling apartment on the Upper West Side to care for an elderly couple.

When she arrived in her starched nurse's uniform, ready to listen to her patients' heartbeats with the free stethoscope that came with her certificate, the couple explained that they had a real nurse already, but could use a cleaning woman with the ability to save their lives should the need arise.

Enide was disappointed but was convinced that cleaning the couple's apartment would be no worse than wiping spittle from their mouths or emptying bedpans.

She traded her starched nurse's uniforms for black tentlike dresses in which she cooked, cleaned, and ran errands for several years until she and Luis had enough money saved to turn their American dream into reality.

They leased a space on bustling Atlantic Avenue between a car wash with a shimmering sign and an apartment building so tall you could have fit an entire village in it.

The neighborhood featured men in platform shoes, sweeping ankle-length furs, and garlanded hats. Their bell-bottom pants were accented with belt buckles that depicted an assortment of ferocious animals: lions, panthers, tigers, twins seated back to naked back, their slender legs raised just so.

The women were perpetually perched at the edge of sidewalks, their short skirts barely covering their thighs. They chewed gum like cows chewing cud, blowing bubbles as big as the moon and as pink as flesh. Luis and Enide christened the place Enide's Caribbean Kitchen. They woke up early every morning to boil pots of black beans which they served over heaps of rice.

As time went by, however, the customers started to order french fries instead of fried plantains. They wanted clam chowder instead of the goat stew Enide took great care to prepare. They asked for hamburgers and Salisbury steaks instead of Luis's asopao and yucca balls.

Enide was reluctant to modify the menu at first; she was downright insulted. But when she realized how much less time it took to make North American food, she gladly acquiesced. Boiling bulletproof beans took hours; hamburgers took a fraction of that time. The new menu made it possible for husband and wife to sleep in and dream their American dream a little longer—instead of rushing to the restaurant before the sun even thought about rising.

The American menu also proved more lucrative; it took at least two hamburgers and a large drink to do what a single bowl of goat stew could do. With the profits, Enide and Luis eventually bought a brownstone on Bedford Avenue. Their neighbors spoke as many foreign languages as they did at the United Nations.

The brownstone had three self-contained units, two of which Enide rented—but only to newlyweds. If you were under thirty and unmarried, Enide Joseph would look through you and give you an unapologetic "Sorry, no vacancy!" Young married couples made the best tenants, Enide reasoned. Between their work and lovemaking schedules, there would be no time to wreck her property.

She and Luis occupied the top floor, which offered a panoramic view of the world below.

Enide and Luis were successful, even by American standards. The air they breathed was sweeter than the apple pie they served at their Caribbean restaurant. (The guava cake had ceased to be an item on the menu.) Their American dream would have lasted a long time too, if someone hadn't barged into the restaurant and shaken them awake in a rather rude manner.

Luckily, Enide and New York had gotten to know each other so well by then that she knew to empty the cash register into the gunman's bag quicker than a zandolit can jump on a young girl's bare neck. Enide even managed a quivering smile, beguiling the thief long enough to keep him from pulling the trigger.

By the time she remembered to conjure up another smile on behalf of her husband, it was too late. The robber had seen Luis's gold watch and decided he could not leave without it. Luis resisted, but the thief had the determination of a condemned man—nothing mattered but the damn watch. He fled with a bag full of money and the gold watch, as Luis's life spilled onto the floor.

"Luis!" Enide wailed. By then her husband had already bled the memory of his own name.

Luis died with an aggravated look on his face. The po-

lice took a report and said, "Sorry about your husband."
They cordoned off the restaurant, declaring Enide's
American dream a crime scene.

The paramedics put the body in a black bag, hoisted
it onto a gurney, and carted it away unceremoniously.
Enide chided herself for abandoning the original Caribbean menu. How could she have been seduced by the
idea of five-minute meals? Fast food had no place in her
kitchen. Had she not given in to the customers' reckless
demands, and kept on preparing the goat stew with okra
thrown in, Luis might still be alive. It was the burgers,
the fries, and the fizzy soda pop that lured the gunman.
Surely he wouldn't have shot her husband over a glass of
guanabana nectar.

"Thunder strike me down!" Enide roared. Things
would have been a little more manageable had Luis been
sick for a while and death asked to be let in. It was the
abruptness of it all that was so caustic, burning her like
battery acid. She pulled herself together quickly, though.
She was accustomed to being separated from the men
she loved. Heartache, the fly that was constantly in her
soup, had become a member of the family.

Burying Luis nearly killed her. Despair threatened
to crush her. A lesser woman would have retreated behind a wall of silence, but Enide made up her mind to
keep breathing and thriving and living. The only question was where.

She had lived in Brooklyn too long now to consider
returning to Haiti. The brownstone was her tropical island now, her new patrie. She paid allegiance to it daily.

The rent she collected covered her mortgage. The
check she received from Luis's life insurance would sus-

tain her for the rest of her days. She would not have to work to support herself; the last thing she wanted was to go back to some old couple's home to wipe backsides and spittle that dripped from mouths frozen into permanent frowns.

All Enide needed was someone who was half as capable of fixing things around the brownstone as Luis had been. Someone to take care of the tenants' occasional complaints without it costing her a fortune.

The answer came within the question: who better than Patrick? The same son she had consigned to some unlit alcove in her mind; the one who took to shining strangers' shoes in order to earn a few extra dollars to feed his wife and child. His little girl, Yseult, looked just like him. Same chin. Same nose. Same black eyes that seemed like they could peer through the ground into the roots of trees.

Enide would have been proud—except she'd never been inclined to have anybody's child refer to her as *Grandma*. But the possibility of Yseult calling her anything at all would be minute; Enide had no interest in ever meeting the child. She planned to send for her son only; wife and daughter could join that growing colony of left-behinds. As far as she was concerned, mother and child could stay on the island till trumpets announced the end of the world.

Enide hired an immigration lawyer and instructed him to do whatever was necessary to get her son to her as soon as possible. Patrick would take Luis's place. He would be useful to his mother for once.

Enide would teach her son about the city's fickle

ways. She would take him to busy subway hubs to demonstrate how to negotiate crowds without bumping into anyone. She would show him how to keep his head down while on the train, so that no one accused him of staring. She would take him to employment agencies and remind him to thank them for any job they offered. She would instruct him to save his earnings instead of squandering it on loose women and flashy clothes. And even if the city ultimately curdled his American dream as it had done hers, he still stood to achieve more in New York than he ever would on the island. Enide's only prayer was that Patrick would not miss that wife and girl child of his. But that was exactly what happened.

As soon as Patrick arrived, he started to pine for his wife. He turned down his favorite dinner on so many occasions that she had him seen by her physician. Weight just slid off Patrick. His face started to sag and his stomach touched his back. He blamed his job at a meat plant for his lack of appetite, but Enide knew better.

Sometimes Patrick kept her up all night, playing sappy bolero music from Luis's old record collection. Those sad songs flooded his bedroom and overflowed into the rest of the apartment. The man could not wait for his wife and daughter to join him.

Enide pleaded with him not to send for them. "It's too soon," she warned. There was still so much he needed to learn about the new country, but Patrick (stubborn as his mother) wouldn't listen.

Enide urged him to wait a few more years, but her appeals evaporated like steam from the bowls of goat stew which Patrick consistently turned down. Patrick sent for his wife and daughter all right. And by some fluke of nature, the consul signed their papers on their first try, allowing them to come.

Enide bit her tongue as Patrick welcomed his family at JFK. She had barely met the woman before Patrick married her. And she had never seen her grandchild. Now her suspicions about how she would feel were confirmed: she despised them both on sight.

Six months after Yvette set foot in the States, she marched right over to Rigsby's bakery to apply for a job. *I live across the street*, she wanted to say, but didn't know how. She took Yseult along. The child's ESL teacher had taught her enough to get a job at the UN. For now, however, Yseult would function as her mother's interpreter.

"Tell him I had my own catering business in Haiti. Tell him I earned a certificate from Madame Blanchard's culinary institute." Yseult translated quickly and accurately.

"I couldn't hire you even if I wanted," Rigsby explained. "The position involves more than just baking cakes." He looked askance at Yvette as he waited for Yseult to translate. When the child was done, Rigsby said: "My customers speak many languages, but in here we speak English. I need an employee who can find out what they want. How they want it. Someone to take phone orders. Understand?"

Yseult translated again. Yvette kept her eyes on Rigsby but spoke to her daughter: "Di misye mèsi pou ryen."

"Mama said thank you." Yseult left out the "for nothing" part. Yvette took Yseult's hand and started toward the door.

"Just a minute," Rigsby called out. Yseult and her

mother turned to face him. "It'll be tough for you to get work if you can't speak English. Like playing rugby with your hands cuffed behind you." He shrugged. "And you can't take your daughter to work with you every day. Anyway, shouldn't she be at school?"

Yseult translated only part of what Rigsby said. She omitted the part about school.

Rigsby crossed his arms and carefully appraised Yvette with his eyes. "My janitor is out again. He's been doing that a lot lately. Jamaican guy. Headstrong." He shook his head as if to ask, *What else can you expect?*

Yseult translated and then nodded to let Rigsby know he could continue.

"You can have his job, if your papers are good." He gave a faint smile. "What the hell? You seem like a nice enough lady. Job's yours if you want it. Starting now." He checked his watch. "You could be deaf and dumb and still be the best janitor in Brooklyn." He indicated the mop leaning against a wall. "Say the word." He flashed Yvette a gold-speckled grin.

Yvette eyed the mop resentfully. She did not wait for Yseult to translate this time. "Di misye lan mèd. Tell him I had my own rèstavèk in my country." Her pointed stare told Rigsby she was not interested.

Yseult was about to translate when her mother cut in: "I didn't leave the island to become a rèstavèk in Brooklyn."

Rigsby didn't need an interpreter to tell him he was being insulted. He moved closer to Yseult and brought his face just inches from hers. "Tell your mama to kiss my ass." He enunciated the command impeccably, then snapped his mouth shut. He waited for Yseult to translate, but the child's face just scrunched up instead. Rigsby took the opportunity to throw in a few more suggestions: "Tell your just-come mama to wake up and smell the fucking coffee. She's not in Haiti anymore. This is Brooklyn, New York, baby! Tell your mama that unless she's her own master around here, she's gonna have to be somebody's slave. Be a good girl and tell your mommy that for me, won't you, sweetie?"

The words had flown too high and fast for Yseult to catch. She decided against asking him to repeat them slower. But with her mother waiting edgily to understand what the man had said, and with Rigsby waiting for Yseult to hurry up and relay his message, Yseult decided to make up something else, knowing that neither would be the wiser. She turned to her mother and muttered in Creole, "The man said thank you for coming to his store. He said if you don't find a job soon, you can come back and try again. Especially after you learn to speak English. He said he'll be happy to hire you then."

"Ten choo veree much," Yvette replied in her best English.

"My pleasure." Rigsby gave a mock salute. "That's the last piece of free advice you'll get in this city."

Yvette held Yseult's hand tightly as they walked back to the brownstone in silence. Yseult's mind floated to Haiti. Cabane Choucoune. She was standing at the gate looking in. Flora was next to her, saying something she could not hear.

Yvela was there too, holding her book bag. Tourists were splashing in the pool, laughing. The tourist-wives looked pretty with their hats and bathing suits emblazoned with ferns. Yseult tried pulling her hand out of her mother's (all that hand-holding made her feel like a little kid), but Yvette tightened her grip.

Several months later, the wife of one of the downstairs tenants came to apologize for being late with the rent. The baby in her arms shook a rattle absentmindedly.

The tenant asked for the landlord, but as usual, Enide was window-shopping in Manhattan, her favorite pastime. The woman then asked for Patrick, but he was at work. Finally she handed the check to Yvette along with her apology. The sympathetic look in Yvette's eyes prompted the woman to share her dilemma: she needed a job to help her husband with the bills, but the high cost of day care forced her to stay home. Of course, the woman did not dream of asking her landlord's daughter-in-law to watch her baby. That would have been disrespectful. It was Yvette who offered to keep the child for a fraction of regular day care costs.

The woman accepted Yvette's offer and shared the good news with friends who were in the same predicament. Within weeks, Yvette had half a dozen babies in her care, earning more money than she would have at Rigsby's bakery.

Yvette surrounded the babies with a wall of pillows to keep them from falling off the bed. She sang soothing lullabies until they all fell asleep. Then she went into the living room to watch *Family Feud*. Richard Dawson, the show's host, intrigued her. Every time Richard puckered his lips to kiss a contestant, Yvette shook her head disapprovingly. This kiss-on-the-lips-in-public business was new to her.

In Haiti, people met, got married, and had babies

all day long. There was plenty of kissing and everything else going on, but no one did it in public. Except at that wedding reception she catered once: during the newlyweds' first dance, the bride had thrown her head back in such a way that said she didn't care who saw what. She had pressed her hips against the groom, pulling him into her white dress. Together, they glided across the dance floor like a wave in the ocean. The bride's movements were slow and deliberate, as if she had danced this dance before. The groom was just as oblivious to the stunned guests. He whispered something in the bride's ear that caused her to bite her lower lip. Her eyes sparked like a struck match. And before anyone knew what was happening, the bride had locked her mouth on his. When the groom shut his eyes, the guests let out a collective gasp. And when the bride closed her own eyes, some of the older guests nearly fainted.

Yvette had been embarrassed for the couple, wondering how they could disgrace themselves so. And even now as Richard Dawson puckered his lips to kiss the contestants, Yvette wanted to turn her head, but then that would have meant missing most of the show.

Enide walked in and began stomping around angrily. "You think money grows on trees? My electric bill has doubled since you came. That TV is on twenty-four hours a day."

"What are you saying, Enide?" Yvette's voice quivered like a child in a locked closet.

"You've turned my house upside down. The showers you take last so long my water bill has gone through the roof. The food in the refrigerator disappears faster than I can buy it."

Yvette turned the TV off and started toward the bedroom where the babies were still sleeping.

"Look at my kitchen!" Enide hollered. "Look at all these baby things. Am I running some orphanage here?"

"Enide, I know you don't want us in your house." Yvette fidgeted with her hands. "Patrick is trying to get us our own place. We'll be gone soon enough."

Yvette went to her bedroom and shut the door. She wanted to dive into the peacefulness that enveloped the sleeping children.

Enide raged on for a while longer before showering and putting on that brown and white dress that still fit nicely over her hips. She smoothed down her afro and wore the hoop earrings that accentuated her high cheekbones.

Enide was still pleased with the face that looked back at her in the mirror. If the men in her life didn't have such a habit of disappointing her by dying (or whatever), she might have taken a fourth husband. She often thought about it, especially after Patrick sent for his wife and Yseult. He was supposed to be her companion, but now he was planning to abandon her. All he did was work, work, work—struggling to save enough money to find a home away from hers.

Enide consulted the mirror one last time and caught the only thing that was lacking in her appearance: the gold Our Lady of High Grace pendant which Luis had given her. She had taken it off the night before when she lathered her hair at the kitchen sink. Where was that pendant now? Enide searched everywhere, but could not find it.

She didn't bother to knock before walking into

Yvette's room. "Have you seen my necklace?" The question came out like the accusation it was meant to be.

"Non." Yvette straightened her spine in another futile attempt to disguise the jumpiness she always felt around Enide.

"I bet your daughter took it."

"Yseult is not a thief." Yvette stepped out of the bedroom, closing the door behind her. Both women were now in the living room.

"Didn't say she was. I'm sure she just wore it to school. To show it off to friends. You know children."

"Yseult is not *children*."

Enide checked the red polish on her fingernails. Satisfied that not one was chipped, she turned her eyes back to her daughter-in-law. Tears were already boiling in Yvette's eyes.

"Calm down." Triumph lifted the corners of Enide's mouth into a smile. "It's not Yseult's fault either to want what doesn't belong to her."

"If she took your necklace," Yvette conceded, "I'll make sure you get it back. When Patrick gets home, I'll tell him. He'll straighten this out."

"So what if Yseult borrowed her grandmère's necklace. Why upset your husband with such a small thing?" Enide studied Yvette's face. When it seemed about to dissolve completely, Enide announced that she would be out for the rest of the day. She took her purse and hurried out of the apartment.

Enide told the cabdriver to take her to Woolworth's in Manhattan. She asked him to go by way of Atlantic Avenue. She wanted to see the old neighborhood.

A Chinese takeout now occupied the space where her

Caribbean restaurant had been. The car wash had gone out of business. The population of pimps and hookers had thinned out some. The taxi veered onto Flatbush from Atlantic, toward the Manhattan Bridge.

Enide thought about Luis, the bleak days after his death. All this reminiscing would be cured by a couple hours of mindless shopping.

When they reached Woolworth's, Enide opened her purse to pay the fare. As she pulled money from her wallet, her Our Lady of High Grace pendant also came sliding out. She let out a little gasp, remembering now the moment she had dropped the necklace in her purse before washing her hair.

She paid the driver and put the necklace back in her wallet stealthily—as if it did not belong to her. As if she had stolen it.

As soon as Enide left the apartment, Yvette went into Yseult's room to search for the necklace. She rummaged through her daughter's things.

In Haiti, Yvette had left her daughter in Yvela's care. The rèstavèk must have turned her child into a thief. When Yvette was not baking a cake for someone's special occasion, she was in bed. In the dark. Listening to those cassettes Patrick sent. Listening to the sad songs and her husband's sad voice. Those songs must have turned Yseult into a thief.

When the consul signed the papers that allowed her to see her husband again, she did get a little distracted. Was that when Yseult turned into a thief? Or did it happen when they arrived in New York? Those first few days when she and Patrick barricaded themselves in their bedroom, wiggling like worms and giggling like children. She had taken her eye off Yseult then. Was that when it happened?

As soon as Yseult arrived home, Yvette tore open the girl's shirt collar. "What'd you do with it?"

"With what?"

"The necklace. Enide's necklace. Where is it?"

"I didn't take Grandmère's necklace."

"Yes, you did."

"I didn't. I swear."

"You swear?"

Yseult nodded.

"What'd I tell you about swearing?"

Tears formed in Yseult's eyes.

"When did you turn into a liar?" Yvette ripped the backpack from Yseult's shoulders, emptying the contents on the floor.

"I don't have it." Yseult's voice broke.

"Then pick up this mess on the floor."

Yseult stuffed her things into the book bag and ran to her room.

Enide's taxi pulled up just as Patrick was walking toward the brownstone. She paid the fare, removed the necklace from her wallet, and slipped it into her front pocket.

"Patrick," she called out, surprised and glad to see him getting home so early for a change. He was seldom at the apartment anymore, working double shifts at the plant, scrambling to save enough money to get his own place.

Patrick kissed her on both cheeks. She tucked her hand into the crook of his arm.

"You look hungry," she said, remembering the days when she used to prepare his dinner. That was before Yvette insisted on making her husband's supper, robbing Enide of one of the few remaining simple pleasures she had left.

Upstairs, they found Yvette on all fours, sweeping her hand under the couch. She looked up when Patrick greeted her: "Your mother said Yseult stole her necklace." Yvette rose to her feet.

"I would never accuse my only grandchild of stealing."

Patrick shook his head, offering a tacit apology for his wife. Yvette grunted her frustration. Enide shrugged her indifference and started toward Yseult's room. Patrick followed his mother.

Yseult was standing near the window directly opposite the door, looking at the street below. Patrick placed a hand on her shoulder, as if to keep her from jumping out. He realized suddenly that she was taller than the last time he had paid attention to such things.

"Did you take Manman's necklace?"

"Non." She did not turn to face him.

"Good." He sounded tired.

Enide stepped to the side of her granddaughter's bed, letting the necklace slip down to the carpet. She kicked the pendant into a shoe under Yseult's bed.

Patrick hoped that Yseult had not stolen his mother's jewelry, but he admitted to himself that his little girl had become a young woman without him noticing. He wondered in what other ways she was different. Leaving her in Haiti had started a separation that continued even though they now lived in the same home. He left for work before dawn and usually returned long after she went to sleep. Sometimes he did not see Yseult for days.

There was something different about her every time he saw her: her eyes were older; her legs had shot up like cornstalks. Had she become a thief too, without him noticing?

He remembered Enide's advice against sending for Yseult and Yvette. His mother had said that New York was a place of opportunity, but it could also be antagonistic and deceitful, offering you happiness with one hand and snatching it back with the other. Perhaps he should have listened.

Enide smoothed her grandchild's hair. "Don't pay any attention to that mother of yours. The necklace will turn up. I'm sure of it." She kissed Yseult and then shuffled out.

Days later, things returned to normal in the apartment. The giggling babies were thrilled to see their day care provider again. Richard Dawson was back in the living room, kissing contestants and announcing, *"Our survey says!"* Patrick went to the meat plant, as usual, working back-to-back double shifts. Yseult went to school. Enide resumed her therapeutic window shopping, asking the cab driver to go by way of Atlantic Avenue occasionally.

One evening when the family gathered at the dinner table, Patrick announced that he had found Enide's Our Lady of High Grace pendant.

"I knew it was here somewhere," Enide exclaimed with an enthusiastic clap of her hands.

"Where was it?" Yvette inquired nervously.

"Under Yseult's bed." Patrick fixed Yseult with a hard stare. "It would have been easier if you'd just told the truth."

"It's quite all right," Enide said. "I forgive you."

"I didn't take it," Yseult mumbled.

Yvette eyed her daughter disdainfully. "When did you turn into such a liar?"

"Take it easy," Patrick said to his wife. "Can't you see the girl is sorry?"

"Yes," Enide echoed, "I'm sure she'll never do it again."

"You never did things like that in Haiti," Yvette blasted.

Yseult lowered her head in defeat. She excused herself from the table and went to her room. She took out her sketchbook and drew two girls on opposite ends of the world; their arms reaching toward each other, but not touching. When she fell asleep just before dawn, Yseult dreamed about Flora.

Across the hall, Yvette pressed her body close to her husband's, whispering: "I cannot live with your mother another day."

THE DISAPPEARANCE
OF YVELA GERMAIN

Don't stare. Pretend you don't see her. Fè kòmsi ou pa wè-l. She acts like her head is hotter than a heap of burning tires, but there's nothing wrong with that woman. Those antics are all part of a brilliant plan. That crazy-beggar strategy has worked successfully now for years. It's still working. Otherwise she'd be dead.

See how she spins around, shaking her bottom like a hooker high on bell tea, flapping her elbows like a bird with broken wings—all this in front of a church. Nothing in Haiti is sacred anymore.

Slick as a dyablès she is. How else would she get away with what she's doing? It takes more than intelligence to hide in the wide open like this. It takes a lot to disappear before everybody's eyes.

She does look like a bone that some stray dog gnawed on and kicked around, doesn't she? Oh, but you know what they say: every bone in the street had flesh once. Trust me when I tell you that *that* woman had flesh. Flesh and everything else that comes with being richer than a dozen dictators strung together.

You name it, she had it: the house, the servants that ran around like red ants in a cane field. She had the chauffeurs and the automobiles that cost more than human heads. All that and beauty queen looks too—courtesy of some million-dollar plastic surgeon—though it is impossible to tell that now.

She used to strut around the katye, swaying her hips like nothing in the universe could bother her. Every day was New Year's, with new dresses and shoes to match. They called her Madan Blan, you know, White Man's Wife. But her name was, or should I say *is*, Yvela Germain.

People bowed down before Madan Blan. She was worshipped. Peasants and gentle folk alike dropped down on their knees to petition her. Yvela Germain was their own Lady of Perpetual Help—the patron saint of every fish vendor who daydreams about commanding a little respect someday.

Yvela herself came from nowhere. No one had ever heard of her people. Judging from her shade of black and those slanted eyes, she probably came from Jeremie or somewhere in that region.

From what I understand, she was a rèstavèk for some time before she decided she'd had enough and hopped on a boat that took her most of the way to Miami before the bottom broke from the top. They sent her to Club Guantánamo. She pickled there for a few years before they kicked her back this way. After all that nastiness, she still managed to marry well and get her hands on more money than there are Haitians under the sea.

But look at her now. Look at her face. That hair is filthier than a pig giving birth. I thought she went back to her husband's country after that night in '99. I thought her husband's enemies caught up with her and arranged a second honeymoon in Hell. But one Sunday morning after Mass, who do I see on the steps of Saint Pierre with a tin cup in her hand, shaking it, and whispering, "Please, please, tanpri souple," like a genuine beggar? Pitit, I almost swallowed my tongue. Back when Yvela Germain *was* Yvela Germain, the house she lived in sat on the most prized piece of land in Puits Blain. The salon alone—with its gold chandelier—was a sight straight out of Versailles. The rooms glowed while the rest of Puits Blain suffered from chronic blackouts. And even though she was an X-signer, you could have searched the entire island and not found a better library than the one Yvela had inside her house. Never spent a minute in anybody's school, but you wouldn't have known it. She had finesse, class, and everything else Haitian royalty keeps behind their monogrammed gates.

The swimming pool, wider than Grand Rivière, boasted a mosaic of amber and mother-of-pearl. Yvela's house was the new Pearl of the Antilles! Ridiculous.

The island must have looked like a buffet through her windows. The panoramic view extended all the way down to the Caribbean Sea.

That woman had upstairs maids, downstairs maids, kitchen maids, and yard people who kept her gardens blazing year round. That husband of hers had more security guards than the Atlantic Ocean has souls. But that didn't stop his enemies from getting him.

Consuelo. That was his name. Looked just like that American actor too. The one from that *Scarface* movie. That was Consuelo. Tèt koupe! Gold-plated skin and megawatt eyes to match. His friends called him "Lolo" for short. We simply called him by what he was: Blan Panyòl.

Lolo had just come back from his country when his servants killed him. They had been watching him board his private jet to come and go in and out of Haiti as if the sky, the sea, and the breeze all belonged to him. He loved Haiti. Couldn't get enough of the sunshine, the poverty, the sadness, the rum, the women, and the young boys who ran around selling whatever it was he wanted them to sell. Then those same boys went around mowing one another down with guns on loan from the big boss. Yes, they watched Consuelo for a long time. Watching and burning to get him.

Blan Panyòl wasn't in that house one night when they rose up against him. They demanded every ounce of *La Chose* they knew he had brought back from the other side.

Like a fool, he resisted. I guess he'd seen too many Al Pacino movies. Yes. Al Pacino—that's the one. Anyway, Consuelo should have handed over every crumb of La Chose he had stashed in that house. He should have dropped down to his knees and begged those servants to spare his life. He should have washed their feet with his expensive cologne and used a pile of his silk shirts for towels. But no.

Lolo was spoiled. He was used to having his way all the time; used to being the one giving the orders. So they tied him to his own bed and whipped him like a runaway rèstavèk. They turned his house upside down, searching for La Chose.

They slashed couches, mattresses. They went from room to room, stomping on Yvela's good rugs, ripping her expensive drapery. They ransacked her library of unread books. They blew through that house like Hurricane Flora herself, destroying everything in their path until they found what they wanted.

The men returned to the bedroom to teach Lolo a final lesson. Watching Yvela bleed would rip him apart, but she had already blown out of that house like a hurricane herself, disappearing like a black bird in the night sky.

Yvela fled Puits Blain and didn't bother to knock on anybody's door to ask for help. She didn't waste time begging anyone to let her in. She knew we would have turned her away. What else could we have done? We'd all seen the vengeance heaped on Good Samaritans. Remember King La Chose down in Port-au-Prince? Didn't his hacked-up corpse stay out there for days until it went up in smoke with the rest of the garbage? His own mother didn't claim him. Let the dead bury their dead. That's the motto I live by around here, especially when La Chose is factored in.

Anyhow, Yvela must have run like her feet were on fire, so fast that her feet never even touched the ground. Taptap drivers on their way home from the city said they saw her galloping down the road like a headless horse. No one stopped for her, of course. Why invite trouble? We all knew what went on in her house.

Yvela probably ran out of breath when she reached the steps of Saint Pierre. Or maybe she just figured that burying herself under a pile of beggars was as smart a getaway as flying to Madagascar or some other sanctuary.

That woman was always very intelligent. How else do you end up in the best house in Puits Blain, when you come from stock that's worth less than a pinch of salt at a fish market? How do you end up being driven around by personal chauffeurs in cars painted to match your fingernail color, when your last ride was a donkey?

Yvela Germain had a good brain, all right. First she got Consuelo to crown her queen of his castle. Then, when the usurpation was underway, she managed to come out unscathed. She vanished by burying herself under a clump of beggars. Who would have thought to look for her on the steps of a church, shaking a little tin cup, begging?

Even I thought she'd left the island. For good. The morning when I came out of Mass and she stretched out her hand to me, begging in a little voice, "Please, please, please, tanpri souple," I reached into my purse and gave her a gourde. I didn't recognize her at first. She was back-alley filthy and smelled like she'd never been within ten kilometers of deodorant. But there was something different about this beggar. It was in the way she tilted her head back; in the ki te mele-m, blasé manner she shook that tin cup. She was new to the streets. Anyone could see that. And still plenty good looking too. In a behind-the-bushes sort of way, but good looking just the same.

When I gave her the money, she lifted her head slightly and I caught a glimpse of her face. She jumped back and fixed her eyes on the ground. But I'd seen enough to know that it was Yvela Germain, Blan Panyòl's wife. She recognized me too, because she scuttled backward like a crab in hot sand and joined the other beggars, knowing that she would be as untouchable as a pearl in a bag of maggots.

The ones who killed her husband searched for her for weeks after that night in '99. They even knocked on my door to ask if I'd seen her. I told them, "How am I supposed to know where that woman is?"

They left and went to pound on other doors. They're probably still searching for her. And look. Yvela Germain is here, hiding in front of everyone. Don't stare, I tell you. Act like she's just one of the other beggars. Pretend you can't see her.

DRIFTING

That's Miss Fatou. I see her every morning on my way to work. She's always sweeping the patch of sidewalk in front of her hair braiding shop. She pauses when she sees me coming. Her blue and gold boubou billows in the breeze. Ma Tante Anna had the same regal disposition, the same plump arms, and the same raw sugar complexion.

Ma Tante Anna would have looked pretty in Miss Fatou's boubou. In all the years since I left Puits Blain, I still cannot picture her in anything other than that stiff karabela housedress she wore every day.

We used to sit on the porch on Sundays, listening to the radio. Ma Tante Anna would turn the volume up when her favorite song began to play. "*Bonswa na di yo,*" she'd harmonize with the singer. "*Greetings to you all.*"

"*Bonswa, Kongo,*" I'd sing with her. "*Greetings to the Congo Queen.*"

Then Ma Tante Anna would take the hem of her housedress between her fingertips, holding the stiff karabela as if it were a flowing Martinique skirt bordered with miles of ruffles and lace. She would raise the housedress just so, revealing once shapely legs. As the music played, Ma Tante Anna would twirl on the tips of her toes, swaying her hips gracefully from side to side.

"*La Reine Kongo nan baryè a*," she'd pipe in her unwavering alto. "*The Congo Queen is at the gate. Take off your hats and bow down*."

When the music ended, Ma Tante Anna would collapse in her rocker. She would catch her breath and fan her face with her hands. "I'm too old to dance the Kongo," she would heave, but if the deejay played the song again, she would take the hem of her housedress between her fingers and twirl on her toes once again.

The night before I left Haiti, Ma Tante Anna looked across the room at me and asked, "Who will sit on the porch with me and sing 'La Reine Kongo'?"

"I will," I said. "Every summer when I visit."

"You'll never come back to this country again." We both fell asleep with those words lingering like shadows in the room.

When I kissed Ma Tante Anna goodbye at the airport the following morning, she shook her head in the disbelieving way mothers do just before they bury a dead child.

Manman was standing next to me, waiting to snatch me out of Ma Tante Anna's grip. Ma Tante Anna paid no attention to her and held me in her plump arms long enough for ten generations to live and die before she let go.

"Good morning," I say to Miss Fatou. She holds the broom still, straightening her spine. She's a tall woman with impeccable posture and charcoal eyes that appraise the hotel uniform on me the way Ma Tante Anna would have.

"Morning," Miss Fatou replies with an appreciative

nod. In her hands, the broom handle is a royal scepter. Her intricate braids look so much like a crown that I resist the urge to curtsy.

When I walk past, Miss Fatou resumes sweeping the little piece of sidewalk under the awning that bears her name in shimmering curlicues. The swish-swishing of her broom follows me as I continue toward the train station.

The kiosk next to the station sells newspapers, cigarettes, and lottery tickets. As usual, I buy a newspaper and a Powerball. A dollar and a dream is all I need, right?

I put the lottery ticket in my purse with a silent prayer that luck might crash into me this time, even if the statistics claim that I have a better chance of getting struck by a unicorn in a lightning storm. Twice.

Reading the newspaper makes the hour ride to work go faster—not that I look forward to another eight hours of taking orders, carrying hot plates and cold drinks, getting yelled at by customers no one could ever please, scraping dirty dishes, smiling, smiling, always smiling, saying "Yes ma'am" and "Yes sir"; praying that customers leave a decent tip; praying even harder that I hit the jackpot and get the hell out of the hotel lobby bar once and for all.

The headline on the front page jumps to my eyes: an unarmed man was accidentally shot seventeen times by the police. Miguel A. Santiago was thirty-four years old. At which point during the seventeen shots did "accidentally" stop being an accident? *He died instantly*, the reporter writes. What does anyone know about the instant of a man's death?

Ma Tante Anna swore that her soul would sail to the sea when she passed away. She promised to visit me occasionally. She said she would drift between this world and the other—until I joined her. Then we would soar like two helium balloons without a string attached to us, strings tending to get caught in tree branches and power lines.

I can't stop looking at Miguel A. Santiago's picture. Features like his invite me to study them for hours. Eyes like that fill me with a desire to find my sketch pad again. The picture must have been taken on a day when the end of the world was so remote a concept to Miguel that he couldn't even pretend to imagine it. He looks like someone who smiled easily and before whom life appeared as long and wide as the Potomac River.

Miguel must have thought he had many more years left to live. The flare lighting his eyes is still burning in this black-and-white photograph. He probably thought that death was something that only happened to other people—old ones, like Ma Tante Anna. She would have been eighty-nine years old today.

I scan a few more articles—nothing as captivating as Miguel's story. Here's a picture of that housekeeper in California who won the $200,000,000 jackpot last week. She's just beaming with happiness! If the jackpot ever came my way, I'd quit my job and never even think about where rent money would come from again. I'd buy a warehouse with a sunroof and sketch all day long. I'd have exhibits anytime I felt like it. I'd sell my drawings to people who appreciate living artists as opposed to dead ones. I'd hire a team of detectives to help me find Flora. We'd go back to Cabane Choucoune and sit by the side of the pool like I told her we would. We'd dip our toes in the water like the tourist-wives used to do. We'd drink cocktails with little umbrellas in them, and crush those silly things like the tourists did.

"Sak pase, ti chérie?" Ma Tante Anna's face materializes out of nowhere. Her eyes flick open between the news columns. She wants to know how life is treating me.

"I'm here," I tell her with the little voice inside my heart. "One day good. One day bad."

There's no point in trying to read the newspaper when Ma Tante Anna visits. Nothing to do but chat with her until memories unravel like the stitches in the karabela housedress she's still wearing. She waits patiently as I become a child again. Here I am now, galloping toward the porch in Puits Blain, calling out, "Ma Tante Anna. Ma Tante Anna." It's morning. She's straightening the creases in the bedspread.

"Look what I found." I open my hand to show her the gold coin. After a stern lecture about picking up objects that don't belong to me, Ma Tante Anna wants to know where the coin came from.

"My friend told me where to find it."

"What friend?"

"The old man."

"What old man?"

"He never says his name."

"Yseult Joseph, what'd I tell you about talking to strangers?"

"He's not a stranger. He talks to me all the time. At night. After you fall asleep."

"What does he say?" Her eyes are wide and expectant.

"He talks about the grove."

Ma Tante Anna circles the room like a moth around a lightbulb. "What else does he tell you?"

"He told me he'd leave a coin under the tamarind tree for me. He told me to scoop the dirt with my hands. So I went to the grove and scooped the dirt with my hands. Look, Ma Tante Anna." I give her the coin.

A smile lifts the corners of her mouth as she examines it. "The ja!" Ma Tante Anna breaks into a combination of tears and laugher. "He gave you the ja." She lifts her arms toward the sky, crying out: "Mèsi Etenèl. Thank you, God." She wipes globs of tears with the hem of her housedress. We're alone in the house, but she closes the bedroom door and shutters the window. No one else must know.

In a hushed voice, she tells me that I must never breathe a word about the ja to anyone else. "Never."

"I won't tell." I etch a sign of the cross on my lips with my fingernail to make the vow official.

"Come," Ma Tante Anna says, taking my hand. She leads the way to the grove. When we reach the tamarind tree, she tells me to keep my eyes open for anyone coming. Then she drops to her hands and knees, muttering mindlessly as she digs. "Are you sure the old man said the tamarind tree?"

"Oui, Ma Tante Anna," I say for the billionth time. "Maybe someone else took the ja."

"The ja was given to you. No one else can just take it." Ma Tante Anna continues to search. She finds a few rusty tin cans, an old pot. She throws those things aside angrily.

We search all day for more coins. Ma Tante Anna complains that the old man is a lot like the ancestors who come in dreams sometimes with instructions they know she's much too preoccupied with everyday problems to decode. Like the time her long-deceased father gave her a number in a dream. She played that number in the lottery for seven days straight; nothing happened.

We search the grove every day for a week, finding nothing. One Sunday afternoon when Ma Tante Anna and I are sitting on the porch and "La Reine Kongo" begins to play, I wait for her to start dancing, but she does not.

"*Bonswa, Kongo.*" I try to entice her into taking the hem of the karabela housedress between her fingertips, but she turns the radio off instead. "Don't you like the Kongo song anymore?" I ask her.

After a long pause she says, "The ja's been in the grove for generations. I was not supposed to help you look for it. It was meant for you alone. I've probably ruined your good luck for life." She shakes her head.

"No one can take my good luck now," I remind Ma Tante Anna. "The consul gave Manman and me visas to join Papa in New York. We're leaving the country, remember?"

"Yes," Ma Tante Anna sighs. "Your good luck hasn't even begun."

"Excuse me," says a man squeezing his way into the vacant seat next to me. He pulls a legal pad out of his briefcase and starts to scribble furiously, filling page after page, pausing occasionally to chew the top of his pen or scratch his head. He seems nervous, careless, someone who might allow things to stay wherever they fall: a matchbook, his underwear, a girlfriend.

The man looks at me suspiciously. His eyes swivel with confusion. I wonder if he can see Ma Tante Anna towering over me, waiting to unravel another memory.

The man says nothing. He lowers his eyes and starts to scribble again.

Ma Tante Anna says, "When you reach New York to-day, kiss your papa for me. Thank him for getting you out of this place. There's nothing here for young people these days, nothing for old ones either. Unless you find a ja, you spend your life in misery and you die hungry." Her eyes are just as sad as the day she decided to stop searching for the ja in the grove. "Be a good girl," she whispers. "Don't let New York change you. You have a good mind. That's why the old man revealed the ja to you. He's been coming to this house for years. He stands in the doorway, but never says a word to me. The minute you showed me the gold coin, I knew. I should have made you shut your mouth. You weren't supposed to tell anyone what the old man said. Not even me. You would have found that ja by yourself, but I couldn't wait."

"Don't be sad," I tell Ma Tante Anna. "The old man will let me know where to find another ja. This time I won't tell anyone, not even you."

"You get only one chance," Ma Tante Anna says wist-fully. Then she starts to half-sing and half-moan a song I've never heard before—about ropes binding her arms and a river overflowing with tears.

"Don't pay attention to the little boys in New York," she continues, "they'll only bring you trouble. And the little girls will only want to steal your good luck. But if you study hard, you won't need luck. If you study every day, you can become a nurse or a secretary. You won't need a ja then."

"I will be a nurse and a secretary. Then I'll come back to Puits Blain and build you a pretty house with an upstairs, a balcony, and running water so that you don't have to go to the well every time you want to bathe or cook dinner."

Ma Tante Anna smiles a sad smile. "Don't wait too long. I might not be here when you get back."

"You'll be here," I tell her just as the conductor's announcement fills the train car. I fold the newspaper that I was not reading into my bag, jumping out of the train seconds before the doors snap shut behind me.

As I walk toward the hotel to start another long shift, I wish I could go back to that morning, years ago, when I found that gold coin under the tamarind tree. I would not say a word to Ma Tante Anna. Maybe there really was a treasure under that tree. Even now as she walks beside me, as quietly as a butterfly on my shoulder, I want to ask her why she took me to the grove that morning when I showed her the coin. I didn't know then that I was not supposed to tell anyone, but she knew. And she knew she was not supposed to burrow the earth for something that belonged to me, but she did. "You didn't ruin my luck," I said to her, but even then I knew I was lying.

WAITING

They hang around here like variables in unsolvable math problems. I tell them my name, Yseult. The tag pinned to my uniform makes that announcement superfluous, but I tell them anyway. "I'm your server," I explain. But they know that too.

They snap their fingers. I bow my head, nice and low, the way the manager likes it. The way Ma Tante Anna used to bow on the porch on Sunday afternoons. She would hold the hem of her housedress and sing along with the radio: *"Bonswa na di yo. Greetings to you all! The Congo Queen is here. Bow down."*

Music trickles down from concealed speakers in the ceiling and walls. An old Billy Joel song seeps into the room. The piano notes are crisp and sweet like apples picked from a mountaintop orchard. The music wraps itself around the customers, slowly and methodically—like a snake.

Billy's voice is unwavering, persistent: *"Don't go changing . . . I love you just the way you are . . ."* Everyone knows the lyrics, but no one utters a word. Clear as the sudden impulse to go skinny-dipping in the rooftop pool, stronger than the conviction that this time they might actually be able to walk on water—"Go ahead, you can do it! *If anyone gives you any trouble, tell them the worm inside the tequila bottle sent you*"—they resist the temptation to belt out the tune. They bob their heads instead, in a slightly inconspicuous way, while the song—like surreptitious love—transforms them.

They hang their heads over empty glasses, remembering the things which the drinks were supposed to help them forget: a son's wrestling match, the out-of-tune but "Hey, that's my daughter up there!" solo in the choir; opening night of the hard-won role in the school's production of *H.M.S. Pinafore* or whatever it was that the letter that came home had said; the tedious arguments that spilled onto quiet cul-de-sacs, letting the neighbors know that love did not live there anymore.

Others scan the room for those who are dying to be found. Eyes swivel frantically as the need swells to a level so urgent that the least bashful among them touch themselves. The monsters in the dark closets strapped to their backs need accomplices willing to make the year's latest version of love. No matter what the critics say, sex with a stranger still has infinite appeal. The danger of it. The thrill!

Danger slows time down. And they like it when time slows down while they're still miles away from their front doors, worlds apart from the other till-death-do-us-part half, far from noisy neighbors' peeping eyes and nanny-cams no one can figure out how to shut off.

They give themselves permission to stray, long before the opportunity presents itself. Culpability, temporarily disguised as bliss, is etched on their faces even before they find accomplices with whom to do the deed.

They snap their fingers, and I run to their tables with

my pen poised on the little notepad with the bar's logo on it. "May I take your order?"

The manager is watching me again, making sure that I show all of my thirty-twos.

"Smile, smile, smile!" the manager tells me all the time. "If I hear one more word about you sucking your teeth, pointing to things with your bottom lip, and mumbling Creole curses under your breath, bye-bye. Guest satisfaction is paramount; that's our motto. Oh, and quit tapping your pen on the notepad like you've got better things to do. Every other server in this place understands that guest satisfaction is what we strive for, why can't you? This isn't some revolution, it's your job. If you're too proud to serve people, then quit. Get back on the boat that brought you here and paddle your way back to whatever little village you couldn't wait to leave. If you want to keep your job, memorize our motto. There's nothing worse than serving Campari when a guest specifically asks you for Midori. One more mistake like that and you're gone. Once you take an order, smile before walking away. Always smile. Somebody's scotch-and-soda may be the difference between paying your rent and being evicted. If you botch it up, it's your baby pictures on the sidewalk. Not mine. Understand? Oh . . . and if you can't do as I say, Miss Baby Doc with the lips stretched out to here, you can always put a dollar on the lottery. But unless you know some strong magic, don't bet on collecting any jackpots. You have a better chance of running into a kangaroo on Constitution Avenue."

I get that pep talk all the time. "Yes sir," I tell the manager. What else can I say? Until I walk out of his five-star shanty, I'll continue to bow my head the way

Ma Tante Anna used to bow when she danced the Kongo. I'll spin on my heels between tables the way Ma Tante Anna used to spin when she danced.

The guests want their drinks faster than the bartender can pour them. What they don't know is that the bartender is drunk, a nasty, creepy kind of drunk. And he has the shakes again. If I rush him, he'll throw sugar into a customer's scotch, which would cost me my job. So I approach the bar god reverentially; smiling twice as obsequiously as I do for the patrons. I give him the order: one Benedictine in a snifter (for the college professor in the sky-blue shirt and paisley bow tie); one cucumber martini (for the woman in the peek-a-boo top); a twelve-year-old scotch (for her companion); one sex on the beach (for the preppy who looks so young I had to card him); a glass of water (for the preppy's friend with the five-alarm fire in his eyes).

They must have met only recently (the sex-on-the-beach and glass-of-water pair). Their love must have just hatched. And now they're standing outside the cracked shell, confused. Those boys' feelings must have sprung up like a clump of daffodils under a bridge, amid sheets of old newspapers and department store circulars. No one planted flowers under the bridge, but they're there. Flourishing!

When I deliver their drinks, the guests take turns reading the name tag which the manager insists I wear. They pummel me with the usual questions: "That's not an American name, is it?" "You're not American, are you?" "Where are you from?" "Has anyone ever told you that you have an exotic look?"

I smile and move on to the next table.

"Darling, isn't she quite the exotic creature?" says Twelve-Year-Old Scotch to Cucumber Martini. "How do you say your name?"

I give him my no-speaking-English look and smile like the manager says I should. "May I bring you anything else, sir? Ma'am?" I smile again. He takes this as an invitation to keep bothering me.

"What an exotic name you have!" He stares at his girlfriend. She rolls her eyes and finishes her drink in two great gulps. "Sweetheart," the man continues, "isn't she an exotic creature? Like one of those new bird species they found in the jungles of . . . Indonesia, was it?"

"Darling, you're flirting with the waitress?"

"This isn't flirting. You call this flirting?"

"I'm going to bed." She holds the empty glass by the stem between two fingers, then turns to me and says, "Send a bottle of Dom to my suite when you're done fraternizing with the guests."

"Yes ma'am." I throw in a half-curtsy.

She looks at the old man. "Come up when you're through." She struts to the elevator and ascends swiftly.

"Good riddance," the old man says. He's looking at me now. "Hey, sweetheart. My little exotic bird from faraway places. Has anyone ever told you that you've got great teeth? Tell me, where is it that you're from?"

"Haiti." I don't need this conversation, but I don't need the man to complain to my manager either.

"Ah. Haiti. Yes. The poorest nation in the Western hemisphere."

So, he's familiar with the sobriquet. "You've been there?"

"Never had the pleasure." He sighs in a theatrical way. "Your country is a sad, sad place."

I smile mechanically. It's my job to smile.

"Wish I could do something to help the people down there."

The way he says "down there" reminds me of that Dante book I started to read fifteen thousand years ago but have yet to finish.

He continues: "Whenever I see your people in the news, my heart breaks. The children get me right here." He pounds on his chest. "So hungry. Diseased. But beautiful. Their eyes. Their lovely eyes. Burning with hope. Burning."

I keep smiling.

"And how long have you been here?" he asks.

I clear my throat and then throw out a number that shaves a decade off the truth. I have a question of my own: "Would you like the drinks charged to your granddaughter's suite, sir?"

"My *what*?" The conversation ends abruptly. He waves me away. He finishes his drink and leaves. When I clear his table, I find a penny under the glass. Big tipper!

I dart among the other tables, making sure everyone's needs are met. I smile at the guests. But I don't stand at their tables long enough for the questions to come. It's the questions that bother me, reminding me of things I'd rather forget.

Once the last guest leaves, I split my tips with the bartender: seventy-five/twenty-five. I throw in the penny from the old man's table as well. Then I find my way to the employee exit. I hit the streets with my uniform, name tag, and apron still on. I'm too tired to care about anything. My back aches. My neck hurts from holding my head up. My face hurts from smiling nonstop. The soles of my feet throb from galloping between tables. I shut my eyes and listen to the muffled rumble of the train. My stop is third from the last. I've got a long way to go. Nothing to do now but rummage through the memories inside the dark closet strapped so securely to my back that I carry it everywhere.

PART IV

SAGESSE

PILGRIMAGE

The morning sky was still night-black when they reached Léogâne. The sputtering flame of tin can lamps lit the worn, winding paths under their tired feet. They had walked for several days and nights, stopping only to sleep by the side of the road. They were not afraid of the dangers that could meet them in the dark. They would have devoured anyone who tried to thwart their mission.

When they reached their destination at last, they saw that there were thousands more like them: men and women dressed completely in white, the customary dress code of miracle-seekers.

Those whose legs could not support them stretched out on sisal mats or the bare mountaintop. The young ones who came because an adult had dragged them along waited anxiously for the pilgrimage to take them back to their own beds that were not damp with morning dew.

"Sove nou, Gran Mèt," the congregation thundered and whirred like the voices of a hurricane. Marianne joined in: "Save us, God. This day." She reached over and touched her daughter's face. Sagesse looked at her manman and managed a trembling smile.

The preacher shouted into his megaphone as he

moved his free hand about excitedly. He stomped his feet and pumped his fist at the sky. In Creole he said: "We will not leave this place until God's favor pours down like rain upon us. We will praise God's name without stopping. The Bible says, *Ask and ye shall receive.* My brothers and sisters, let us ask until our voices give out."

The preacher took a deep breath before continuing: "Some of you crossed dangerous roads to reach this place today. Some of you had to trick the enemy to get here. For many of you, getting to this mountaintop was in itself the miracle. Your perseverance will be rewarded today. The doors of deliverance will open. Misery's yoke has been broken. The enemy is defeated. This, brothers and sisters, is the day God delivers us from the malefactors' web of wickedness. We will taste victory today. If you believe this to be true, somebody say amen."

The congregation responded with a roaring, "Amen!"

The preacher went on: "Tap the person next to you. Look him or her in the eye and say, *Neighbor, you will taste victory today.*"

Sagesse would not have looked into her manman's eyes even if she were tall enough. No child on the island would have been so bold. Instead, she tugged on Marianne's white blouse, saying, "Neighbor, you will taste victory today."

Sagesse was fourteen years old. Every year since she was two, her mother had taken her on a similar pilgrimage. She had become very good at playing her manman's *neighbor*.

Marianne pinched her daughter's cheeks playfully. "Neighbor, *we* will taste victory today!"

When the preacher announced that special blessings awaited those who prayed with their whole hearts, Marianne dropped to her knees and flung her arms wide open, palms poised to snatch whatever crumb might fall out of the sky. Faces touched the ground. Lips kissed the dew. Everyone was now singing at a pitch as piercing as the hunger that was sure to grip them by noon. Marianne sang with them: "*Kapitèn bato minote yo.*" Sagesse threw her voice in too: "*Captain of my ship, bind my enemies and drown them deep in the sea.*"

Sagesse was all the family Marianne had. The woman who claimed to be Marianne's manman had sold her to a couple in Port-au-Prince. The couple never thought Marianne was worth twenty whole US dollars. The child was more than a little careless at times. She got up at five to fetch water every morning, but spilled most of it on the way back from the stream. She had trouble holding the five-gallon drum on her head like other rèstavèk children. Marianne also prepared breakfast for the couple, but the liquid she tried to pass for coffee was too often undrinkable. "Because of you," the lady of the house would say, "we've wasted a ton of good coffee. You'll work here until we recover every penny!"

Marianne was six years old when she learned to wash white and dark clothes in separate buckets—after being told to do so countless times, of course. But her hand would slip occasionally. Drops of indigo would fall into the water and turn the white clothes a pale blue. Bleach would drip onto a pile of dark clothes and ruin them. "You're a useless thing," the lady of the house would remind her.

Marianne ironed the couple's clothes and bedsheets, but she burned holes in just about everything. She could never get the proper amount of charcoal in the iron's chamber. The lid never quite closed. Bits of lit charcoal would fall on one side of a garment and come out on the other. "You're dumber than the dog," the lady of the house would scream. But Marianne never thought the dog was anything other than kind; it slept next to her in the kitchen shed every night.

The girl was an awful cook too. Even at eight years old, Marianne could not figure out just how much salt to put in a simple pot of beans; it was always too much or too little. The couple wanted to return their rèstavèk; trade her in for a better one. They wanted their twenty US dollars back too. They asked around but could not find the woman who had claimed to be Marianne's manman.

The couple did what they could with their unwanted rèstavèk. They beat her daily, but even that was futile. They kept Marianne until she was too old to be told what to do: twenty-two. Then they packed her things (a couple of threadbare dresses), threw them in the street, and told her to leave—but not before the husband had raped and impregnated Marianne.

"Sè la vi," Marianne said when her règle stopped, her breasts swelled, and her belly got so big that she could not see her own feet when she looked down. "Such is life."

Pregnant and homeless, Marianne would have died on the streets of Port-au-Prince. But an angel intervened.

Yvette, who was pregnant herself, ignored her husband's warning and opened her home to a stranger. She offered Marianne her own kitchen shed. "Stay as long as you need," she said.

Marianne did not have to cook Yvette's meals. She did not have to iron bedsheets. When she attempted to wash Yvette's clothes one Saturday morning, the woman pulled the basket out of Marianne's hands, saying she had one rèstavèk already. She did not need two.

Marianne kept Yvette company when her husband was at work. Yvette was glad to have someone there—a friend who listened to her questions and concerns about her unborn child. *Will it be a boy? A girl? I hope she's born with five fingers on each hand. I hope she has two hands. Two feet. I hope she's not blind. I hope she loves me. I hope labor isn't as painful as they say. I hope my bones spread apart easily to let the child through.* Marianne had the same questions but kept them in her heart. The baby would be what the baby would be. Sè la vi.

Marianne and Yvette ate plantains, salted herring, and white rice on the front porch every evening. Afterward, Yvette sat like a child between Marianne's knees. "You have good hands," Yvette often told Marianne. "My hair has grown since you started combing it."

"It's the lwil," Marianne would say. "It makes hair grow fast."

"Tim tim?" Yvette would pipe up excitedly.

"Bwa sèch!" Marianne would answer, knowing what would follow.

"My mother has four children," Yvette would say. "When one is not home the others might as well be gone."

"Four tires of a car."

Yvette would smile. "Tim tim?" she'd say again, hoping her new friend would not know the answer to the riddle.

"Bwa sèch!"

"Kapitèn behind the door?"

"Broom!" Marianne would not hesitate. The answers would fall out of her mouth. She knew them—though no one had taught them to her. The answers were in her blood.

"Tim tim?"

"Bwa sèch!"

"Kapitèn under the bed?"

"Chamber pot."

The women would go on for hours, stopping only after Yvette's husband came home and took her away.

Both women had girls.

Marianne named her daughter Sagesse. Yvette named hers Yseult.

Morning, noon, and night, Marianne now sat on a rock behind the kitchen shed and washed clothes while Sagesse cooed nearby. She hung the clothes to dry on lines that crisscrossed above her head. When the sun went down, Marianne got up and filled her iron's chamber with charcoal. She pressed shirts, pants, and bedsheets to perfection.

Marianne's laundry business kept food on the table. When Sagesse started school, the business paid for that too. But Marianne still dreamed of a better world for her daughter—a world which would be possible only by way of a miracle.

Yvette and her family now lived in New York. She sent Marianne a cassette whenever someone she knew traveled back to her part of Haiti. Yvette said the country was not easy to live in, but there were more opportunities for children to make something of themselves.

Marianne prayed that Sagesse would not spend her life on a rock behind somebody's kitchen shed, washing strangers' clothes from sunrise to nightfall. Her prayer went unanswered for years. Pilgrimages were futile. The mountaintops were barren deserts that exacerbated her thirst rather than quenched it.

The mountaintop above Léogâne was different. It yielded ripe fruit without the unbearable wait between planting and harvest seasons. After years of petitioning the consul at the American Embassy, he finally stamped his consent on the stack of documents in Marianne's hands. He even wished her luck.

Marianne feared that her miracle would decompose and attract flies like dead fish under the noonday sun. What if the consul changed his mind and asked for his visas back? What if a cruel wind blew the kitchen shed and her visas away? What if she'd been dreaming? Marianne carried all of those *what ifs?* with her to the nearest travel agency and traded her life's savings for two one-way plane tickets.

The prospect of moving to New York filled Marianne with so much joy she could not stop singing.

She sang as she sat on her rock behind the kitchen shed doing the last load of laundry. Years of ringing heavy karabela fabric had withered her hands, but she did not feel the pain today. Everyone who passed by wondered what there was to sing about. As soon as Marianne told them, they understood.

Marianne sang as she parceled out her belongings to those who came to haul away everything the New York–bound duo could not take with them.

"Going to New York is a lot like dying," someone quipped. "You have to leave all of your possessions behind."

"I'd pitch my thirty-two teeth down the latrine," Marianne shot back, "for a chance to live in paradise." Tacit consensus and the clicking sound of goodbye kisses filled the shed.

Marianne continued to sing as she packed what was left of her things in a small suitcase. She sang as she locked the shed one final time. She sang during the tap-tap ride to the airport in Port-au-Prince. In the airplane, during the flight to JFK, she sang softly the one song for which Sagesse never cared:

> Ti Zwazo, where are you going?
> I'm going to Fiyèt Lalo's
> But Fiyè Lalo knows how to eat children
> If you go, she will eat you too . . .

Marianne used to sing that song to Sagesse whenever the child disobeyed her. Ti Zwazo turned bad children into good ones. It made them stop using the food on their plates as toys; it made them change into their everyday clothes as soon as they reached home from school or a pilgrimage. Ti Zwazo made children do their homework every night without being told. It made them swallow spoonfuls of cod liver oil without a word of protest. Ti Zwazo had power. Marianne went on singing:

Ti Zwazo, kote ou prale
Mwen prale kay Fiyèt Lalo
Fiyè Lalo konn manje timoun
Si w ale la manje ou tou . . .

The song took on a life of its own inside the airplane. Halfway to the new country, an entire section had "Ti Zwazo" on its lips. Those who were familiar with the melody only, hummed along. Sagesse sang with them, predicting her own future without knowing it.

Frozen raindrops pummeled their heads as they left the airplane. Marianne's old benefactor Yvette picked them up from the airport.

Yvette brought two overcoats in which Marianne and Sagesse promptly bundled themselves, but that did not stop the cold from breaking through their skin and lodging in the marrow of their bones.

Yvette teased her friend: "Congratulations, dear! Here is the New York you dreamed about. Here is your miracle. The fun is just starting too. It gets better. Wait until you have to stand at a bus stop in below-zero weather. Your own toes will curse you." Marianne was shivering too much to say anything.

Yvette gave Marianne and her daughter a room in her row house on Nostrand Avenue. "Stay as long as you need," she told them, knowing that Marianne would not be able to pay until she found a job, which might not happen for months. Maybe a year.

"Stay as long as you need," Yvette repeated. The words comforted Marianne. "This country is not one you'd want to be homeless in. It gets so cold here the ground freezes. People freeze to death, if you can believe such a thing."

Marianne's mind drifted. For a second she was back on the streets of Port-au-Prince among the homeless newborns, old people, and every age group in between. She recalled pacing the streets with an unborn Sagesse in her womb. She recalled the nights when she slept standing up or on cement slabs in cemeteries because the sidewalks were too crowded. Marianne remembered the days she went without food. There were no soup kitchens, no shelters with one-cot-per-person hospitality. There were no street-corner trash bins with half-eaten treasures buried in them. No such luck on Port-au-Prince's ruthless streets.

"Yvette Joseph," Marianne said to her friend, "thank God for you. You saved my life once before and now you're doing it again." And then to Sagesse: "You see, girl child, lamitye se lò! A good friend is better than gold."

Yvette's husband, Patrick, agreed. He was thrilled that Marianne and Sagesse would live with them. Sagesse was the same age as Yseult, their daughter.

"She refuses to make new friends," Patrick said of Yseult. "Sometimes she goes for days without eating. Everything is *Flora this* and *Flora that*. She stays in her room like a prisoner." He hoped that Sagesse would draw Yseult out of her self-imposed solitary confinement.

Sagesse tried to make friends with Yseult, but the girl was not interested. She went out of her way to avoid Sagesse. When a meeting was inevitable, Yseult met Sagesse's greetings with barely perceptible nods or with curt responses in a tone that shouted *Go away!*

Sagesse was fresh from the other world. She was available for friendship with anyone who didn't expect her to speak the strange new language. But since she wasn't Flora Desormeau, Yseult Joseph could not care less.

Yvette babysat a couple of preschool children during the day, but her real job didn't start until the kids were picked up by their parents in the evening. The *real* job's only stipulation was outlined in an unspoken agreement: several thousand Haitians in Brooklyn would pay her any amount of money in exchange for firing up her oven and baking the gato that transported them back to the island with each bite.

There were only two kinds of Haitians in Brooklyn, Marianne soon learned: those who bought their gato from Yvette Joseph and those who didn't. Marianne looked for work during the day. In the evening, she helped Yvette in the kitchen. If that woman ever stopped making gato, an angry mob would gather at her front step with picket signs.

Sagesse was enrolled in the same high school as Yseult, but they were not in the same classes. When they ran into each other in the hallway, Yseult would dash off in the other direction, lest Sagesse say anything that required more than a quick nod in response.

Yseult feared nothing more than a conversation with Sagesse. There were moments when she did want to speak to Sagesse but could not think of anything to say. With Flora Desormeau, she never had to speak. Her friend always knew what she was thinking and feeling.

Yseult did not think it possible to miss anyone as much as she missed Flora. She did not believe—until the very last moment—that the two of them would be separated by so great a distance. It was one thing to know that one day she would take a plane and leave Haiti. It was something altogether different to say goodbye and walk away, never to see or speak with Flora Desormeau again. Leaving her best friend was tantamount to having both arms severed. What good were a hummingbird's wings if one was one place and the other thousands of miles away?

Nine months after Yvette picked up her friend from the airport and teased her about her miracle finally coming true, Marianne found a job. One of Yvette's customers knew someone who knew someone who knew a couple of rich ex-pats who needed a live-in maid. The only problem was the couple lived in some remote town in New Jersey.

"That's not a problem," Marianne said. She was eager to discover other parts of the country.

The well-off ex-pats for whom she would work said it was fine to bring her daughter along. "The servants' room is huge," the lady had said.

"And Sagesse can help with chores when she's not in school," Marianne heard herself offer. Finally, she thought, she would begin to make her own way in the new country.

Yvette pleaded with her friend to stay. The gato business was better than ever. Birthdays, baptisms, first communions, confirmations, graduations, weddings, real estate transactions, retirements, and funerals all required special gatos, but now customers wanted them for no special reason. "I just feel like having a slice," they would say. In addition to gato, they also wanted pen patat, pate, akasan, batonè. The business was growing steadily and bringing in enough profit to justify opening a bakery.

"We'll work together," Yvette told Marianne.

"I need to make my own way," Marianne countered.

"We'll be partners," Yvette said.

"Thank you, but—" Marianne shook her head. She could not tell her friend that Brooklyn and its Konpa Dirèk music pulse was a little too much like Haiti for her taste. She loved Creole, but longed to hear a little less of it. She was, after all, in a different country.

"I'll visit as often as I can," Marianne smiled. She could not know that she would never see Brooklyn again—not because anyone would prevent her, but because she would not wish to. And Yvette would always be too busy baking gato to go anywhere.

Yvette kissed her friend goodbye. They held each other for a moment and a lifetime of memories filled the space between them. Perhaps they would run into each other one day. Perhaps they would not. Their time had come and gone. Their friendship, precious and uncommon, would be there waiting for them to resume it—if ever one needed the other again. But for now, this was goodbye.

When Yseult heard the news, she cornered Sagesse in the hallway between classes and looked deep into the girl's eyes as if they'd known each other all their lives, as if they'd been friends. "Sagesse," Yseult said in a barely audible voice, "are you really leaving?"

"Yes."

"This is for you." Yseult gave her a tattered notebook.

When Sagesse opened it, her own eyes stared back at her. Marianne was sitting next to her on the wing of a large airplane. Both were in oversized winter coats. Even in the pencil sketch the figures seemed to be shivering. "You drew this?"

Yseult nodded.

Sagesse looked through the pages and found women with baskets of merchandise on their heads, men wielding machetes in cane fields, stoic policemen with rifles like babies in their arms, a rèstavèk standing on the shadow of letters that spelled the name *Yvela*. There were pages and pages of two girls frozen in a game of oslè. "These are incredible." Sagesse's eyes were wide with admiration. "You're a great artist."

Yseult dismissed the compliment with a wave of her hand. "Every Haitian is a great artist. We just have different art forms. What's yours?"

Sagesse shook her head. "I don't have one."

"Sure you do," Yseult said, and produced a second notebook. "Maybe you're a poet. A writer? You can write stories."

"I don't know any stories."

"Sure you do," Yseult insisted. "Every Haitian knows at least one story worth telling. And with a name like Sagesse, you probably know many." Yseult gave a shy smile. "See you at the house." She ran away.

Later that day, Sagesse went to Yseult's bedroom to thank her for the notebooks. She had looked at the sketches again and was amazed by Yseult's talent. The people in the notebook seemed to be alive. Yseult had captured the finest lines on Marianne's face—as if the subject sat for hours under a bright light, waiting patiently to be immortalized.

Yseult smiled. She had hoped that Sagesse would stop by her room before leaving. Sagesse hesitated in the doorway, raking the space over with her eyes before venturing in. Back in the kitchen shed where she had lived with Marianne, nothing was ever out of place. Their sleeping mats were always rolled up and put away during the day. The bag of ranyon which they layered on the mats to make them a little softer was always under the table, out of the way. Their clothes were clean and folded in bags in one corner. The white pilgrimage dresses hung on a hook in the wall—ready for the next miracle hunt. What did this messy room say about Yseult Joseph?

Everywhere she looked Sagesse saw sketches of places and people. Several stuck out from underneath the pillows on Yseult's bed. The walls were covered with even more vivid drawings. The walls themselves served as canvases. Behind the bed was a mural of two girls on their knees, looking through a wrought-iron gate. There were more sketches strewn on the floor and on the shelf next to her bed. "You really like to draw, don't you?" Sagesse said. It was not a question.

Yseult nodded.

"What inspires you?"

"Life." Yseult sounded like a ninety-year-old woman. Regret swept over the two of them like a blast of cold air. They could have been friends. They could have gotten to know each other, but Yseult had refused to make space for anyone but Flora Desormeau. If she could not have Flora's friendship, she did not want anyone else's.

Sagesse listened to Yseult carefully. She understood her now. The past was her inspiration. Her sketches were her friends. Her heart was safe with them. The girls talked for hours. Yseult led Sagesse to her desk to show her the piece she was working on: a strong female figure with a mile-high afro, large hoop earrings, and angry eyes. The enormous pendant that hung from a heavy chain around the figure's neck had elaborate details. The words *Our Lady of High Grace* were etched around the pendant.

"Who is that?" Sagesse shuddered.

"Enide, my grandmother," Yseult said. "We lived with her when we first came to New York. She hated me. She died awhile back."

"Sorry to hear that," Sagesse replied in Creole.

"Don't be. She lived her life fully. She tried to live other people's lives for them too. Manman wouldn't let her."

"Oh . . ."

"You remind me of her."

"Your grandmother?"

"No. My best friend."

Yseult indicated the only framed sketch on her desk. A surge of happiness passed through Sagesse, making her speak a little too eagerly now: "Flora Desormeau?"

"How did you know?"

"Your papa told me. He wanted me to help you forget her. Said all you did was miss her. I tried to make friends with you, but you didn't let me."

"Papa doesn't understand anything. Flora and I were like this." Yseult hooked two fingers together.

"Where is she now?"

"Port-au-Prince. Up the street. Boston. Miami. Who knows? Before I came to the States, I'd heard that New

York was big, but had no idea how big. Our geography teacher showed us maps, but who knew that New York was a humongous city inside a humongous state that is only one of fifty other humongous states? People don't run into one another like they do in Port-au-Prince. You could live next door to someone and never learn their name. Never even speak a word to them for years."

"Like us. We barely spoke to each other. And we lived in the same house for nine months."

"Precisely."

"But I'm glad we finally did talk—even if I'm leaving."

The eyes that had sparkled only moments before were dull now, cloudy. Yseult's voice broke as she spoke. "I know Flora is in the United States somewhere." Yseult was standing a few inches away from Sagesse, but a wall shot up between them suddenly. Yseult retreated into her secret place like a turtle into its shell.

"Called information?" Sagesse asked.

"Ten thousand times. There are many Desormeaux here. Not the one I need."

"Maybe one of them knows her."

"Maybe. But no one said so. Can't blame them. Everyone is so scared. This country can be dangerous."

"That's true."

"So be careful where you're going." Yseult studied Sagesse's face, secretly itemizing the similarities and differences between her and the best friend etched in her memory.

"Manman said the place where we're going is quiet, which means there'll be little chance of getting into any kind of trouble."

"That's good. Maybe you'll write your stories there."

Yseult smiled. The subject was being changed.

"Who knows," Sagesse said, her voice a little too loud. "Maybe I'll run into Flora Desormeau where I'm going. I'll tell her where to find you."

"That'd be great." Yseult ushered Sagesse out of her room as politely as she had brought her in.

Had Sagesse known that she would never see Yseult Joseph again, she would have thrown her arms around her and told her she loved her. She would have said the words without caring how they sounded. "Mwen renmen-w." She wished she had said those words now as Yseult retreated back into her impervious shell.

Marianne could not wait to leave Brooklyn. Nostrand Avenue with its Caribbean heartbeat reminded her too much of the place she wished she could forget.

Yvette gave up trying to talk her friend into going into business with her. She understood Marianne's reasons for wanting to leave. Besides, Yvette thought, inviting another woman to share her kitchen might have been a recipe for trouble. Marianne might have gotten too comfortable over time; how long before she would have started with the unsolicited advice: *Put another pinch of salt in those beans. Turn the flame down under that rice. Stir those lumps out of the cornmeal.* Wouldn't that have been enough to make one despise the other?

Moving day came and went without fanfare. Marianne and Sagesse packed their bags which were no larger than the ones they had come to the States with nine months earlier. They did not possess any chairs, beds, or tables. Everything they'd used during the last nine months belonged to Yvette, who was now standing over the mixer on her kitchen counter. The thing whirred noisily. "Time to get a new one," Yvette said mostly to herself, even though Marianne was standing nearby. "I'd give my right arm for a good mixer." She sucked her teeth.

"The whole arm, macomère?" Marianne teased.

"Well, maybe not the *whole* arm. Maybe a couple of fingers. Maybe just the pinky. What good is the pinky anyway?"

"Yes, what good is it?" Marianne said. "Can't wear a ring on it, unless you want people to think you're loose. Can't open a can of milk with it. Can't hold it in the air to insult anybody properly."

"Actually, you can insult a man quite properly with the pinky—if you accompany the gesture with the correct words."

"True." A surge of bitterness rose in Marianne. The only man she'd ever known was the one who raped her years ago. It never occurred to her that there was more to men than a bottomless rage skillfully hidden behind starched shirts, cologne, and charm.

"But I think I'll keep my arm and my fingers, even the pinky."

"I think you should too."

Marianne and Yvette were saying one thing when they meant something else, but Sagesse was not interested in climbing their hill of words. She was ready to leave. She had said goodbye to Yseult as well as the room she'd lived in for nine months—like a baby waiting to be born. She had stuck her head out of the bedroom window, listening to the street's heartbeat one last time. She was ready to accompany her manman on the next pilgrimage. Ready to begin the new life which Marianne had found for them.

The rich ex-pats who hired Marianne sent a car to fetch her. Sagesse went in first and greeted the driver in his black suit and hat. Marianne followed, her steps determined and unfaltering.

Had they looked back at the house, they would not have seen Yseult standing behind the curtain, peering down from her bedroom window. She could see out but no one could see in. Yvette was less fearful of saying goodbye. That was a part of life—like breathing and eating. So she stood at the front door, waving the spatula gripped tightly in one fist.

The new town was lifeless. You could walk for miles and not see another person. The houses were far apart and hidden behind impenetrable cypress walls. There was no Konpa Dirèk music wafting out of open windows. The streets were comatose. You could scream for hours and not be heard. There was no Caribbean restaurant or side-street stall heaped with papaya and mango. There was nothing to remind Sagesse of the island. Nothing to remind her of herself at all.

On Saturday mornings, if the sun was shining and a neighbor's maid opened the windows, a somber aria might seep out. At the house where they lived, the ex-pats listened to Charles Aznavour and Chopin. No one else.

Marianne enrolled Sagesse in the nearest public school. "It is much better here than in Brooklyn, oui?" The new bosses' English was often laced with French words. There was no difference in their pronunciation of "the" and "deux"; they trilled the "r" wherever it presented itself. The wife was a French literature professor at some big-time university. The husband was a partner at an international law firm that specialized in mergers and acquisitions. The entire package suited Marianne so well that she went around the house smiling and wearing a dishrag around her neck as if it were a Hermès scarf.

Marianne sang while she dusted furniture so ornate that it must have belonged to a king. Each piece must have been flown directly from some château in France to the ex-pats' own palace in the heart of the Garden State. Marianne sang as she brought the mile-long countertops to a celestial shine. She sang as she baked konparèt in a monstrous oven that looked like it belonged in a restaurant.

"C'est bon!" The couple loved Marianne's cooking. They swore every dish she prepared was better than a trip back to the island they hadn't visited in the three decades since they'd left.

Marianne sang as she cleaned the house nonstop, beating her little drum of happiness like that battery-powered bunny on TV.

Sagesse did not care too much for her new high school. She was the only Haitian there. In Brooklyn she could go several days without uttering a single English word. Most of the teachers spoke Creole and French. Many of them were Haitian. There were countless other Haitian kids at the old high school too. The majority of them spoke Creole. There was no pressure to speak the new language. No pressure until now.

"Bann djou, Sage us," the man said. "Sakee pase?"

Until now no one had butchered her name so. Sagesse wasn't even sure the man was speaking to her. But since she was the only person standing in the doorway, and since the man was looking straight at her, Sagesse thought it best to give a polite nod in response. The handful of students sitting in the classroom behind the man half-smiled in her direction.

The man tried to make Sagesse feel comfortable by speaking to her in the little bit of Haitian Creole he knew, but Sagesse was unmoved.

"I'm your new teacher," the man said with a wide smile.

Sagesse nodded.

"I speak seven languages fluently," the teacher announced. He rattled off the list: "Spanish, Portuguese, Thai, Vietnamese, Chinese, Korean, and Russian, but not too much French or Haitian Creole."

Sagesse nodded again.

"I love Haitian Creole," the teacher went on with a shake of his head, "Plenty of French cognates. But those phonemes . . ." He wiped imaginary sweat from his brow. "Whew!"

Sagesse nodded yet again. She did not understand everything the teacher said, but had a sense that he had said too much.

What the teacher did not share with Sagesse was that he'd once taught in Brooklyn, but had to leave for personal reasons after just a few months. He used to be in Miami too (and left after a few months, also for personal reasons). Boston, Columbus, Los Angeles, Austin: he'd taught in just about every American city with a large immigrant population, but never stayed very long.

His longest stint had been in Thailand. He'd lived there for ten years, teaching English to students in villages throughout the country. He promised himself to return there once he retired.

"I like to move around," the teacher once explained to a colleague. "I'm a single guy, you know, and a straight one at that! It gets to be a little funny in this business for guys like myself, know what I mean?" The colleague did not know what he meant, but nodded and hoped the teacher would go away.

"I can teach anybody to speak English," he boasted. "Young or old, I can teach them all!" More polite nods would follow from colleagues who wished the man would crawl to the nearest landfill and stay there. Sometimes when they smelled him coming down the hallway (he had a strong, utility-closet-self-gratification odor that preceded him and lingered in a room long after he left it), they would hurry off in the other direction. His colleagues did not like him. They did not know why exactly; they simply found it impossible to like him. They knew they would not leave their own children with him for a second; they could not bring themselves to trust him. They disliked his arrogance and the loud voice that disrupted faculty meetings when everyone was supposed to be quiet. His constant twitching and the sucking sound he made with his teeth bothered his colleagues, but no one ever said a word. They were all afraid of him. Afraid of what he might do if anyone stated the obvious.

"One of these days," the teacher told Sagesse, "I'll go to Haiti. I have friends there already. In the countryside. They're having a phenomenal time." Sagesse nodded again.

She was not sure what else she was supposed to do.

The teacher's name was so difficult to pronounce that everyone just called him Mr. E. He had thin lips and straight dark hair with splashes of gray in it. His eyes arrowed to a squint with each smile. And because he smiled a lot, he always seemed to be squinting. He was always meticulously dressed, and his shoes shone like new—as if he'd never taken a step in them.

Mr. E had an odd walk. He seemed uncomfortable on his own feet—as if they did not belong to him. He moved like an injured bird, a hawk, trapped in a man's body. His feet never came all the way down, so he appeared to be tiptoeing. He roamed the school hallways on the tips of his toes, looking for mischievous students.

Alejandro, from Nicaragua, stomped his feet when English words played hide and seek in his brain. Francisco, from Mexico, could spend hours trying to describe the snakes he saw in the desert he crossed in order to reach the States.

Fatima, from Brazil, had bronze skin, arched eyebrows that accentuated her rainforest-green eyes. She had perpetually red lips and a tiny waist that made her look like a living doll. Fatima made a swarm of paper butterflies which Mr. E displayed on a bulletin board. Those butterflies were trapped in the classroom. Their wings were stuck together, useless.

The Latino kids clumped together in gym and at lunch. Every now and then, Fatima and Sagesse would sit together, but not often. Mr. E felt so sorry for her that he said she could eat in the classroom if she wanted. Sagesse liked the idea of being alone in the classroom, but Mr. E never planned to leave her unattended.

Mr. E's classroom soon became Sagesse's oasis. Unlike other teachers who lost their temper when she could not speak the new language fast enough, Mr. E never broke pencils or threw chalk across the room. Instead of punishing his students for not understanding lessons, he celebrated their achievements—however small. He knew how difficult it was to learn a new language.

"Take the verbs, for instance," Mr. E would say. "The regular ones are clear-cut. Just add *d* or *ed* and you have the past. The irregular ones are wacky. There's no logical reason why *go* becomes *went* and *eat* becomes *ate*." The kids were thoroughly confused but managed to memorize the weird verbs anyway. Mr. E was so thrilled he took them out to lunch one afternoon.

Sagesse, in particular, had surprised him with her uncanny ability to retain information. In Haiti she memorized her homework every night and recited it the next day. It took a good memory to negotiate the jagged twists and turns of a new language. Within a few months Sagesse learned enough English to move up several proficiency levels.

"Little Sagesse," Mr. E said one day during lunch period, "I am going to point to something in the classroom and you'll tell me its English name."

"A vocabulary quiz?" Sagesse was ready to show off all the English she'd memorized.

"In a sense." Mr. E pointed to the origami on the bulletin board.

Sagesse said, "Butterflies."

He pointed to the thin, angular thing between the left and right sides of his face.

She said, "Nose."

Mr. E pointed to the chalkboard, the chairs, the clock, the desks, the overhead projector, the floor, and his shoes. Sagesse knew the names of all of those. When he touched the front of his pants and waited for Sagesse to call out the English word, she froze.

"What is it?" he asked again, still touching his pants.

Sagesse had not learned the English word for the thing. "Pijon," she blurted out, taking small imperceptible steps toward the doorway.

"Pigeon," Mr. E chuckled. "How perfectly adorable!"

A few weeks before summer vacation, Mr. E said he would take the class on a special field trip to celebrate how well everyone had done. When Sagesse reached home that afternoon, she told Marianne that the teacher wanted to take the class on another authentic-lesson-in-the-new-culture field trip, as Mr. E called them.

Marianne sighed. Forming words required energy she did not have. Every meal the ex-pats wanted took hours to prepare. No longer pleased with konparèt and akasan, they requested quiches, soufflés, and tortes—the sort of food Marianne did not know how to make.

The husband wanted his underwear ironed. The wife wanted the sheets ironed. Socks had to be folded a certain way. Towels had to be just the right height from the floor. The floors had to be washed—by hand. Daily. "Mops have germs," the wife complained. Pots and pans had to look as if they'd never been used—even if Marianne was the only one who cooked. "And try not to speak so much in Creole," the wife said. "Too much of that in our house," the husband agreed. When Marianne used the few French words she knew, the ex-pats laughed so much that tears fell from their eyes. Marianne had become their rèstavèk. She'd expected her new life to carry a price, so she endured the riotous laughter at her expense, the disapproving looks, the derogatory comments, the paychecks that failed to clear . . . The hunters' children were the ones who enjoyed the catch. Wasn't that how it was supposed to be?

"You have to sign," Sagesse said, and gave Marianne the permission slip for the field trip.

"You sign," an exhausted Marianne replied.

Sagesse scribbled her manman's name as effortlessly as she would have done her own.

"Where are they taking you this time?" Marianne inquired. No matter how many times Sagesse told her that Mr. E was just one person, Marianne insisted on referring to him by the plural *they*. She was convinced that it took a team of teachers to fit into Sagesse's head all the English she had learned.

"The museum. And then a pizza place for lunch."

"Make sure you put something in your stomach before you go," Marianne said. "You don't want them to think you're a greedy Haitian."

"I will."

On the day of the field trip, Sagesse found Mr. E in the parking lot leaning on the van he usually drove the students around in. A school bus should have been rented, but no one ever questioned Mr. E's actions. He was the expert on foreign kids. When other teachers thought the foreign kids were more trouble than they were worth, they sent them to Mr. E's classroom. He would deal with them. Keep them out of the mainstream. "Wish they'd disappear from the test scores," one teacher said. "Why do we have to include them in every damn thing? They pull the numbers down, making us look like we're not doing our jobs."

As far as the other teachers were concerned, the foreign kids were peculiar—weird like the lunches they brought to the cafeteria from home. The less they knew about the foreign kids the better. As long as Mr. E had signed permission slips, as long as the paperwork was in order, he could do whatever he wanted with them.

Sagesse gave Mr. E her permission slip and jumped into the van, securing a window seat before anyone else could.

A few minutes later Fatima dove in like a tiger through a burning hoop at the circus. Mr. E sat down in the driver's seat and fastened his seat belt.

Fatima unzipped her book bag and took out a tube of lipstick. "Want some?" She held it out to Sagesse.

"No thanks."

Fatima shrugged. She applied the lipstick then reached into her bag for an eye shadow palette. She peeled back the cover and rubbed a finger over the deepest shade of blue.

Mr. E started the engine.

"Where are the others?" Sagesse asked.

"Who needs them?" Fatima hissed.

"They're not coming," Mr. E said as he pulled out of the parking lot.

"Give me a hand." Fatima turned toward Sagesse.

"What?"

"Help me with these stupid things." She was trying to glue on false eyelashes.

The storm at the bottom of Sagesse's stomach told her something was wrong.

Mr. E adjusted the rearview mirror for a better look. Fatima giggled.

"How far is the restaurant?" Sagesse had a tremor in her voice. She would run away when they reached it. She would call the police and tell them that her teacher had taken her against her will. But, Sagesse thought, Mr. E would show the police her permission slip. Perhaps Marianne would get in trouble.

"Relax," Fatima said in her molasses accent. "We'll get there in a flash."

"Thank you," Mr. E said.

Fatima rolled her eyes at Sagesse.

"What sort of an expression is *in a flash*?" Mr. E said.

"Idiomatic." Sagesse pinched her own hand so hard it burned. She felt like an idiot who couldn't tell the difference between the classroom and real life.

"Very good!" Fatima was being sarcastic.

"But you should have raised your hand first," Mr. E said. Now the two of them were laughing like an old couple who could finish each other's sentences.

The restaurant was a narrow building near a trash-strewn alley. The stucco was the greenish-black of an advanced mold problem. Rusty accordion grills were pulled back, leaving a slit through which patrons filtered in but not out. The package store to the left was covered with posters of scantily dressed women leaning against giant liquor bottles. The church, next to the liquor store, had heavy chains and a padlock on its doors. Two doors down was a fast-food restaurant with a broken neon sign. Locked inside was a pit bull that was either dead or asleep in a pool of vomit.

"Let's go." Mr. E offered Sagesse the crook of his elbow. She pretended not to notice. Her eyes scanned the area for anyone who might be able to help her.

The music in the restaurant could be heard from across the street. Fatima ran toward the music. Mr. E pushed Sagesse through the front door.

Madonna's "Like a Virgin" boomed through colossal speakers positioned around the cavernous space. Fatima said something in Sagesse's ear, but the music was deafening. "What?" Sagesse screamed.

"I'm going to change!" the Brazilian girl shouted.

"Change?"

She did not answer. She skipped down the aisle and disappeared behind a black door with a star on it.

Mr. E searched Sagesse's face for a reaction. The girl was scared and had a thousand questions which she dared not ask: *Why did the teacher bring me here? Will I become a face on the back of a milk carton? Is this how kids disappear? Have I disappeared? Will I see Manman again? Will Mr. E bring me back home? What will I tell Manman if he does bring me back? Am I supposed to escape and call the police? What will happen if I do? Will they believe me? Will the police believe that I did not know where Mr. E was taking me? Who will believe me? Who can I tell? Manman will be angry with me. She'll be ashamed, won't she? She'll cry, won't she? She'll want to fly back to Haiti and be sad again. And the people Manman works for, they'll fire her, won't they? They'll throw us out of their house. They'll spit in Manman's face. They'll spit in my face. Or maybe they'll help Manman find me. Is anyone looking for me? Am I a missing person? It's my fault, isn't it? Will everyone blame me? I must have done something to make Mr. E bring me here. What did I do to make him bring me here? I shouldn't have said* pijon *when he touched the front of his pants. I should have pretended not to know. It's my fault. I was the one who said the word. That's why I'm here.*

"Relax!" Mr. E shouted.

Sagesse shook her head. She was now on the mountaintop in Léogâne. It was morning. The moon and sun were engaged in their dance of defiance. Marianne was singing the "Captain of My Ship" song, praying for visas while Sagesse prayed for the consul to stamp *Denied* on their application once again. They should have taken a kantè instead of waiting years for their application to be approved. They should have taken a boat, Sagesse thought. Their bodies would have been at the bottom of the ocean now, safe from Mr. E.

It was difficult to see anything through the smoke that enshrouded the room. Clumps of men stood here and there, each one clutching a glass of this or a bottle of that in his hand. Little round tables were strategically placed at the foot of a small wooden platform onto which a crimson spotlight beamed.

The girl on the platform, tall and slender, had jet-black hair that fell to her waist. She moved languorously. A frilly garter hugged the upper part of one thigh into which the men took turns inserting various denominations of money. The girl wore nothing more. She shimmied down, her back sliding on the pole that shot up to the ceiling which was speckled with glow-in-the-dark stars. The girl frowned when she saw Mr. E. He blew her a kiss. She gave him a hateful look before turning away.

"That's Belkis," Mr. E said. "She was one of my best students."

Belkis shifted her hips from side to side, moving her head in a slow, circular motion. Her hair swept the face of a man standing before her with money in his hands. She swung her head around again, turning her face in such a way that the money ended up between her teeth—like a mourning dove with a twig in its bill.

The man walked away as others approached.

"Fatima's next," Mr. E said, as if Sagesse had asked. "Fatima has big plans for her future," he added with a meditative look in his eyes. "She wants to work smart, not hard. She'll make a mint in this business. You can too. It's up to you."

Sagesse did not respond. She focused her attention on the picture of Marianne floating before her. She needed to tell her manman about Mr. E and Belkis and Fatima. Was Marianne whispering something about returning to the mountaintop in Léogâne and requesting a new miracle? Sagesse hummed the old pilgrimage song, changing it just a little: *Captain of my ship, bind Mr. E and drown him deep in the sea.*

One song faded into another and another. When Fatima appeared finally, her hair had changed into a lion's mane. Her lips were lacquered. She had poured herself into a corset that looked wet. Matching short-shorts had one zipper in the back.

Fatima ran to the little stage and swung around the pole, lifting both legs up in the air like a trapeze artist. The men cheered and called out her name. She smiled triumphantly, opening both arms to embrace the dark room and everything in it.

Fatima danced and twirled and moved her hips as if she had done it many times before. The men filled the frilly band around her thigh with money. After a few songs, an exhilarated Fatima traded places with another girl. This one looked as bored and exhausted as a Kanaval queen on the last night before Lent. She took her time getting to the platform, as though each high-heeled shoe weighed fifty pounds.

As if on cue, the audience turned away. The men began to talk among themselves, ignoring the Kanaval queen who bit by sluggish bit removed her regalia.

"Show's over," Mr. E said just as a bowling ball of a woman approached the table where he and Sagesse were sitting. The woman extended a chunky hand with bulky gold and silver rings on every finger. Some of the rings had chains that crisscrossed on the back of her hand and turned into bracelets. "This the new girl?" she asked. "What they call her?"

"Don't know yet," Mr. E replied. "What do you think, Tiny? You're pretty good at naming them."

"She looks like a Ginger to me." Tiny hunched her wide shoulders.

"Then a Ginger she just might be." A smile crept on Mr. E's lips.

"When will you give us the pleasure, Ginger?" Tiny eyed Sagesse expectantly.

"Ginger might need a little help." Mr. E shook something in his pocket that rattled like pebbles in a plastic jar.

Tiny grunted her dissatisfaction with Mr. E's answer. She hated to give the girls "the medication." That was always a little too risky. Some girls would pass out and need to be babysat until they came back around. The ones who got giddy (which was what the medication was supposed to do) could dance for hours without catching their breath.

"Sweet Fatima!" Tiny exclaimed in a dramatic voice. Fatima had changed back into the clothes she'd worn into the place. "You were wonderful, my dear. As always."

The compliment brought a sparkle to Fatima's eyes and a rosier glow to her cheeks. "Thanks, Ms. Tiny!"

"Let's get going," Mr. E said, and ushered the girls out.

Once inside the van, Fatima counted the money she'd made. "Two hundred and seventy-eight US dollars!" she exclaimed proudly. Two hundred and seventy-eight shiny new notches in her belt. Two hundred and seventy-eight little fingers reaching under her arm where the skin is tender, to tickle her until laughter gushed out.

"Two seventy-eight." Mr. E glanced at Sagesse through the rearview mirror. "In less than one hour! Even I don't make that."

Fatima stuffed the cash into her book bag. "My mother doesn't make that much money in a year," she said as she wiped the goop off her lips with the towel that magically appeared from her backpack.

When they reached the school parking lot, Mr. E stepped out before Sagesse could—to block her way. He searched her eyes for a long time before speaking. "Tell one soul about our little excursion today and I'll have your mother deported. One soul." He made a cross on his lips. "The class went to the museum today. That's your story and here's the proof to go with it." He pressed a couple of brochures into her trembling hand. "We had pizza for lunch. It was delicious. And you had fun. Understand?"

Sagesse shook her head as if to say no.

"Yes," Mr. E said. "I know where your mother works. I know the people she works for. One word and you'll be gone. Homeless. One word and you'll beg me to have you deported."

Sagesse nodded. She understood English much better than she thought.

The sun was still in the sky when she reached home. Marianne was in the kitchen scrubbing pots and humming "Ti Zwazo." Sagesse kissed her on both cheeks. "How was the field trip?" Marianne asked in Creole.

"Fine."

"I hope you ate something before you went. I hope they didn't take you for a greedy Haitian."

"I did," Sagesse lied. "Can we go back to Brooklyn, Manman?"

"Never," Marianne replied. "You have a chance to make something of yourself here."

Sagesse said nothing else. She went to her room and took out the notebook Yseult Joseph had given her. She stared at the blank pages. The tap-tapping of raindrops on the window startled her. The sky had been cloudless only moments before.

BOUZEN

The word grew wheels that chased Sagesse wherever she turned. She saw it everywhere; she could not escape its all-encompassing scope. The word latched onto her when she tried to hide, sucking—like a leech—slowly, persistently. The word spawned a brood of winged beings that swooped down from the sky, scratching and clawing at her eyes until they ripped sleep away every night.

During the day the word whirred inside her head, hissing as it lifted, dropped, and tossed her about like a kernel of corn in a windstorm. She avoided her own reflection, fearing that mirrors would tell her the truth. She would find the word etched across her forehead, on her chin, on her cheekbones. Surely, anyone looking at her closely would see the word leaping off her skin—the letters raised like bold scarifications. But scarifications were supposed to beatify, not make the face unsightly.

Sagesse scolded herself for having spoken the word. Saying it just once had brought her face-to-face with Mr. E's clandestine activities and the threats he promised to carry out if she told. She would not risk losing any more of herself by uttering the word ever again.

She would have given an eye to return to that lunch period many years ago when Mr. E pointed to the origami, the clock, the desk, the chairs, and the thing inside his pants. She knew the thing's name, but wished she had kept her mouth shut. How had she learned the word in the first place? Who had taught it to her? The answer was wedged between other volatile memories, growing steadily like a volcano on the ocean floor.

One Saturday morning many, many years ago, a man had come to the kitchen shed with a bag of laundry for Marianne. "Where's your manman?" the man had asked.

Sagesse had seen him countless times before. Marianne had done his laundry for years. He was a good customer; the money he paid helped to keep Sagesse in school, buy her uniform and books. The money helped keep food on the table. Wasn't that what Marianne had said?

Sagesse thought nothing of it when the man had looked to the left and right, then behind him—to see if anyone was watching. "Manman went to the marketplace," Sagesse had told him. The memory always stopped there. Nothing else happened beyond that. The man just disappeared. Or was she the one who vanished? Nothing could jolt the memory of what transpired after the man checked to see if anyone was looking. Not even Mr. E and his threats could dislodge the memory out of the place where it was wedged. But if the memory ever shook loose, she would hear the man say: "When is your manman coming back? I brought a bag of laundry for her to do."

"Leave the bag here," Sagesse had told the man. "Leave it just outside the door. Manman will return soon." The man had dropped the bag by the entrance and stepped inside, pulling the door shut behind him.

Sagesse had retreated to the far end of the kitchen shed, but one leap had brought the man inches from her face. She hid her face behind her hands, waiting for the beast to strike. The man had taken one of her hands away, pulling it by the wrist and bringing it down on something that felt like a small bird whose wings were folded under itself. Perhaps the bird had just been killed, its frail bones steadily hardening.

"You know what this is?" the man asked. Sagesse had kept her eyes closed, her face buried in the crook of her elbow. She never knew what it was that the man made her touch. "It's a pigeon!" Wasn't that what the man had said, his voice in short breaths as if he'd run from one end of the island to the other?

"You like it?" the man had asked, moving Sagesse's hand as if it were a lifeless puppet. Tears had leaked out of her eyes, but the man did not see those. When he was done, he gave Sagesse her hand again—as a parting gift. "Tell your manman about this and I'll find another washing woman. Tell your manman and I'll let everyone know you're a bad little girl who likes to do bad things to men. Tell your manman and I will burn this shed down while you're asleep one night." The man pushed the door, and walked out. He returned many times, always right after Marianne left for the marketplace.

The doctor at the free clinic tried to help Sagesse forget whatever it was she could not exactly remember. The medication worked for years, quieting what the doctor called "intrusive voices." But the medication had triggered an insatiable craving for honey buns. Sagesse would eat dozens in one sitting, pushing them into her mouth, one after another. The weight gain was not enough to deter her; she had never cared about such things. It was the news about Marianne that made her stop taking the medication altogether.

It had been years since they'd left the ex-pats' castle in the Garden State. Husband and wife had migrated to the south of France for a permanent vacation. Marianne found a job cleaning an attorney's office at night. Sagesse attended a community college, taking courses in psychology—even though some classmate suggested that she'd make a better patient. She studied diligently, waiting for the moment when something inside her would click, urging her to make at least one friend instead of being alone all the time. She studied and waited for what the doctor called healthy social behavior, but it never came.

The receptionist who discovered Marianne called security, thinking she had caught a thief hiding under her desk—with a duster in her hand!

"Why, that's Miss Marianne," the security guard said. "I wondered why I didn't see her leave this morning."

Sagesse missed her classes that day. She went down to the morgue to identify her manman instead. Marianne's hands were clutched in angry fists; her face was frozen in disbelief. Sagesse forgot to take the medication that day. And the realization that she was now alone in the world came like wind-driven water seeping under her door, rising and rising until it reached the ceiling—drowning everything in between.

Sagesse did not remember consenting to the autopsy;

what did it matter? It was discovered that Marianne had an enlarged heart; Sagesse could have told them that! Marianne's cremated remains now lived in a small container next to Sagesse's psychology books, waiting like something to be mailed, if only the sender had an address.

SAGESSE

The room was filled with even more smoke than Sagesse remembered. The people seemed to be frozen in time. Nothing had changed since the day Mr. E had brought her there many years before. Some of the men were smoking. Some bobbed their heads in time to the music. Others were reaching out to the girl on stage and stuffing money into the garter high around her naked thigh.

Sagesse walked up to a bowling ball of a woman standing behind the bar and told her she needed a job. The woman took a quick look at Sagesse and said, "You're in luck."

The bowling ball's teeth were yellow, her breath smelled of liquor, her eyes had a vicious look in them. Her clothes were stained with food and drink. The dried mustard flakes at the corner of her mouth must have been days old. She looked dirty, shifty. "Call me Tiny. I run the place." She motioned to a girl who was drinking something brown from a short glass. "One of my best dancers," Tiny declared.

"At your service," the girl slurred, but there was a sober look in her eyes.

"Show this young lady to the dressing room. She's going to audition for us. Maybe join the lineup. If she's half as good as she looks." Tiny grinned. "The suspense is killing me." The bowling ball's eyes were on Sagesse's lips. "Wanna drink?"

"Sure." Sagesse had never had one before. Something about the occasion suggested that it was the perfect time to start.

Tiny mixed a concoction which Sagesse drank as fast as it would go down. A fire lit up inside her and suddenly she wanted to dive into the Caribbean Sea and swim toward the deepest part.

"One more!" Sagesse said, surprising herself.

Tiny smiled as she filled the glass and gave it back to Sagesse, tacitly urging her to swallow the contents quickly. "Take her downstairs," she said to the girl standing behind Sagesse.

Sagesse turned to look at her. She was pretty in a *so what?* sort of way. But her eyes imprisoned Sagesse until the girl decided to blink, setting her free. "Follow me," she said in a raspy voice. Her hair flowed like a silk veil in the breeze, brushing Sagesse gently on the face.

The girl had the calculated stride of a market woman with a heavy load on her head. They walked down the narrow stairway that led into a cavernous basement. It was cold and damp and electrical wiring crisscrossed above their heads. Half a dozen bright globes dangled from the ceiling, illuminating every corner of the room, as well as the thick makeup on the girl's face.

A parrot-shit shade of green covered the walls, the carpet, and the old stuffed chairs. There was a large oval mirror leaning against an old banquet table, its frame also painted parrot-shit green.

"Did you bring a costume?" the girl asked.

"A costume?" Sagesse's mind went back to the Brazilian girl from her old school. She recalled Fatima saying she would change and returning with a crazy outfit on and hair teased to death.

The Ti Zwazo song which Marianne used to sing all the time looped inside Sagesse's head now while the girl talked. Her lips were moving, but Sagesse could not hear anything but the upside-down lullaby her manman would not stop singing.

The girl figured Sagesse was high. She shut her mouth and began to shout with those eyes: *Why are you here? Can't you see this isn't a place for you? I can see this isn't a place for you. I got lost one day and ended up here. I was just passing through . . . on my way to becoming a . . . a . . . I don't remember now what it was that I was on my way to becoming . . . It doesn't matter anymore . . . But I do know that I was going someplace else . . . Not here . . . I got lost and I've been here ever since . . . But you . . . you're a child . . . Get out of this place before the music, the alcohol, the men, and the money all link arms and shackle you . . . Get out before time tricks you into believing you're something you're not.*

"I don't have a costume," Sagesse said.

The girl shrugged.

"Can I borrow one of yours?"

"Knock yourself out," the girl said, and went back upstairs.

Sagesse changed into a little minidress made out of faux leather. She teased her hair and put on too much makeup. She checked the mirror, but did not recognize the eyes looking back at her. Whatever Tiny had concocted was now swirling like a hurricane in her head. She was hot and cold and hot again. She was not sure where she was until she reached the top of the stairs and

Tiny took her hand and pulled her into the deejay booth.

"Gentlemen," Tiny said into a microphone. Her voice was like a sponge filling every crevice in the walls. "I have a treat for you tonight." Tiny turned to Sagesse and asked, "What's your name, pumpkin?"

Sagesse thought for a minute and said, "Ginger."

Tiny grinned as the memory floated to her. She never did forget a face. "Little Ginger here is going to blow your minds, boys!"

The men buzzed with anticipation.

Tiny spoke in a half-sarcastic tone, as she prayed to whatever god she believed in that Sagesse/Ginger had it in her to deliver.

PART V

CASSEUS

PAPER BOATS

Leaning against the dilapidated lectern, Professor Beaulieu surveyed the classroom while adjusting the stiff fixture around his neck that was most incongruous with the sweltering climate.

He smoothed his mustache then slammed his fists on the open book from which he would read the day's selection. The loud thump shot through the students like thunder. Beaulieu grinned. When he was satisfied that his students' faces registered a sufficient level of fear, he unleashed the oft-practiced set of vocal gymnastics that never failed to unhinge his captive audience. He raised his voice here and there and lowered it to a whisper in other places.

Beaulieu spoke in that impeccable French he'd spent years perfecting. He prefaced his lecture with a lengthy warning concerning the inherent complexities of the material he would present: "Plato, in many circles, is a god." He pronounced the ancient philosopher's name reverently. "In *The Republic*," the professor continued, "Plato equates art with idea or reason so indomitable that it thought itself into being. This is not for the feeble-brained." Each time the professor's fist came down on a page, a wave of intimidation spread across the classroom.

Beaulieu scanned the bewildered faces staring back at him. They all looked the same. This recurring thought was accompanied with a great degree of repugnance. He despised the students' vacuous eyes, the gaping mouths.

In Beaulieu's estimation, the students had not changed in the thirty years since he began teaching philosophy at various universities throughout the island. When bright rays of intelligence emanated from one of the faces in the flock, Beaulieu would invest countless hours, trying to brand it his. This semester, however, talent was absent. No one stood apart from the herd. No one, except Jean-Max Casseus, a seventeen-year-old boy who preferred to doze off, doodle, or daydream. Beaulieu had secretly conferred upon him the Future Beggar Award.

Jean-Max was like a splinter under Beaulieu's fingernail; the professor was anxious to dig him out with the sharp end of anything. Jean-Max, the paying customer, had certain rights of which both he and the professor were keenly aware.

As long as the boy's tuition continued to be paid on time, the administration would let him stay at the university for as long as he wanted. Much to Beaulieu's chagrin.

"Plato is not for everyone," Beaulieu went on contemptuously. He resented having to teach a group of boys he deemed utterly unteachable. Not one among them belonged to a respectable family. These were the children of illiterate peasants. Their parents had conspired to spend every cent on providing them with a formal education rather than rearing them to carry on the family tradition of raising chickens and goats or selling fried pig meat from a roadside stall. Perhaps the cost of being X-signers had proven too steep over the years. Perhaps those peasants had lost too many acres to charlatans who'd duped them into carving X's where they should have spat.

Beaulieu longed to work at a school where the population was a little more sophisticated. But this university was the only one paying what he considered a decent wage.

"Scholars have dedicated lifetimes to Plato's work. You boys are fortunate that this subject is being presented by me in such a way that any monkey can grasp it. You boys should consider yourselves fortunate to have me, indeed."

"Woy!" Jean-Max screamed. Every eye in the room turned to him.

"Mr. Casseus," Beaulieu's voice was pricklier than usual, "would you mind explaining to the class Plato's concept of art?" He adjusted his bow tie and smoothed his mustache before slamming his fists down on the lectern. Like hummingbirds flittering mischievously above Jean-Max's head, Professor Beaulieu's words were gone before the student could catch one. So utterly transfixed was he by the scene developing on the road two stories below that he neither heard nor saw his teacher.

The professor stomped his way across the room, stopping squarely in front of Jean-Max's desk. Beaulieu removed his eyeglasses and twirled them violently between his fingers. "Well, Mr. Casseus, I am waiting."

"M-Monsieur," Jean-Max stuttered as he indicated the scene below with his pointing finger, "look!"

The accident had happened so quickly that it looked like a scene in a movie. Were it not for the cacophony wafting up to the classroom, Jean-Max would have dismissed the incident as a figment of his own imagination. But his eyes had not deceived him: a school bus did in fact swerve off the borderless road and plunge into the steep ravine.

"Mezanmi, gade, gade!" Jean-Max screamed. "Come see, everyone, come and look!"

His classmates swarmed the window, shaking and mumbling incoherently; their shoulders stooped with a sudden heaviness. Professor Beaulieu was stunned when he peered down. "What happened?" he asked— not because he could not see the crumpled school bus but because his kind always needed a secondary source to substantiate whatever his own eyes showed him.

"Bòs la tounen tankou yon toupi," Jean-Max described what he saw in breathy spurts of Creole, forgetting that the professor had banned "the peasant's tongue" in his classroom. Only French was allowed. ("Because," as Professor Beaulieu put it, "speaking French lets people know that you're educated. Speaking French well sets you apart from your compatriots who've never seen the interior of a school building.")

"The bus spun like a top," Jean-Max continued in Creole. The professor's French-only rule flew out the window like a bird in an unlatched cage. Jean-Max shook as he spoke: "The bus somersaulted off the embankment several times before plunging head-first into the river. Then it rolled on its side and settled there, half-submerged, as you can see."

Professor Beaulieu nodded. He was not sure how to proceed. Jean-Max and his classmates ran out of the classroom with the urgency of rèstavèks facing a birthday whipping. Beaulieu, befuddled, did not budge.

Jean-Max and his classmates reached the river's edge just as a bloody-faced boy was making his way out of a shattered window. Jean-Max hurled himself into the river with the intention of swimming him to shore. But the boy was so infuriated with the hand fate had dealt him that he thrashed about, pummeling his rescuer with angry fists.

Undeterred, Jean-Max subdued the boy long enough to drag him to shore. He handed him to a classmate who made the boy regurgitate the lungful he had taken of the river. With his first unobstructed breath, the boy let loose a litany of curses at the sky.

One by one, the other passengers began to appear. Most of them were still inside the bus. The driver's body was locked in a macabre embrace with the steering wheel; he had a stupefied look on what was left of his face. Two girls in matching patent leather shoes with little eyelets on the sides held hands as they floated—facedown. The boys, in khaki knickers and white short-sleeves, couldn't have been more than twelve years old. An older woman, possibly the chaperone, looked dignified—even though her skirt was now an upturned parachute floating about her shoulders. One broken leg was frozen in a high kick. The woman's panties, which looked like a deflated beach ball, hung below her hip bone, exposing a scar that spanned her midsection like the border dividing the island's two countries.

The students continued their rescue effort long after it was clear that the boy would be the only survivor. Nineteen children perished in that crash. The oldest was fifteen.

Something imploded in Madan Louisaint's chest long

before she received the news. Her neighbor, Madan Casseus, brought a pot of salted coffee to help reduce the zezisman, but the grief-stricken mother refused a sip.

All day Madan Louisaint had likened herself to a house disarranged—as if someone had ransacked the usually tidy rooms inside her head and heart. All day she'd drifted like an empty shell in a storm. All day she'd sensed that her twin girls would not return home in the same form they'd left. All day she'd regretted letting them board that bus, but the morning sun was halfway done with its daily journey across the sky; nothing could convince it to retrace its scorching steps.

In the years since she'd given birth, Madan Louisaint never recalled the sting of the midwife's blade carving a path for her girls. But that old scar chose to burn as intensely as it had the night she'd pushed the babies out. Madan Louisaint's very breasts behaved peculiarly as well. When her newborn twins had refused her milk, engorgement turned her breasts into stones then too. Only now did she understand why those memories chose this time to slash her with their double-edged blades, leaving her hollow, abandoned—a desolate place where no living thing could possibly survive.

The youngest, Beatrice, had one foot on the ill-fated bus when that chronic stomach pain reared its unforgiving head, making her stay home. How the child had cried!

Had she been on that bus, Madan Louisaint would have lost everyone she had left in the known world.

"Woy, bon Dye," Madan Louisaint wailed. She was standing outside of her own body, looking at a woman doubled over. She could not comfort that woman. She *was* that woman. Such was the pain of losing two children on the same day. At the same time. Her heart had been slashed in two. Each child would be mourned separately.

"Woy, Etènel, pouki sa-w fèm sa-a?" Madan Louisaint could not stop asking the same rhetorical question. Her hands reached up to tear the housedress covering her heaving chest. Sharp fingernails scratched the skin underneath, drawing rivulets of blood. "Why, God, did you do this to me?"

"Pran kouraj," Madan Casseus offered the only words of consolation that came to mind. She, too, had known the lacerating pain of losing a child. "Take heart, macomère." She stroked her neighbor's hair.

"No heart left to take," Madan Louisaint whispered.

Jean-Max returned to the university the following day. The image of those bodies trapped in the bus was still so vivid that he could not listen to anything the professor had to say. Beaulieu's lecture about some long-dead philosopher's concept of reality was painfully irrelevant.

Jean-Max closed his notebook and asked permission to address the class. Professor Beaulieu swallowed hard before consenting.

"We have to do something," Jean-Max began with all the decorum he could muster. "I did not sleep all night."

The other students nodded in agreement. Jean-Max continued: "What happened yesterday gives me problems. It's true we all have to die someday, but those children . . ." He cleared his throat. "Ti moun yo mouri mal. Those children died an ugly death. We have to do something to honor them."

Professor Beaulieu shifted nervously.

"It takes a ja of gold to bury someone on this island. Who has that kind of money? We are poor, but we must honor them."

"Men anpil chay pa lou," a classmate piped up—his eyes bright with optimism. "We'll take a collection. We'll set up tents in every katye to collect donations."

"A collection of what? Stones?" another classmate demanded angrily. "Jean-Max, you just said we're all poor. In case you've forgotten, my friend, you live in a mud hut. You don't have money to give. Neither do we. I lost family members in that crash; other students lost sisters, brothers, nephews. What more do you want us to give?"

"A gourde here," an unrelenting Jean-Max countered. "Fifty cents there. We can mobilize the entire student body, souke kò nou, at least long enough to usher those children to respectable graves."

"I'll go to Pétionville," one student chirped. "I'll go to Cabane Choucoune. That place is always packed with tourists. I'll beg them for whatever they can spare."

"Good!" Jean-Max exclaimed. "We cannot sit here with our hands in our pockets, doing nothing."

Later that day, Jean-Max led a group of students into the marketplace. They stopped before each stall to ask for a donation. The vendors who were thankful that the accident did not claim one of their own prefaced each donation with, "Well, you know business hasn't been good in years." They then reached into bras, tiny drawstring sacks, and shoes to find a crumpled bill or two. An old man in sweat-soaked clothes offered Jean-Max a stack of blackened gourdes that he had collected from a group of charcoal vendors.

Legions of students from nearby schools joined Jean-Max and his classmates in their effort. Collection tents were pitched in every katye. Men and women who heard about the accident delighted in expressing their sorrow.

The most generous contribution came from Monsieur Boursicault. His chain of funeral parlors had made him the wealthiest man in Haiti. "I would be honored to help," he said when Jean-Max approached him. The accident was just the sort of opportunity Boursicault had been waiting for. "I'll take care of the bus victims gratis." He would show his appreciation for the island's loyal patronage by donating the caskets, the flowers, even the burial clothes. He would also supply memorial pamphlets bearing every deceased person's name!

The families accepted Boursicault's unprecedented offer quickly. The bit of cash that Jean-Max and his classmates collected would not have covered Boursicault's steep prices anyway. Now that cash could be used for rice and meat and beer for the obligatory post-funeral feeding.

No church in town was large enough to accommodate the number of people who wanted to express their grief. The families agreed that a mass memorial service would be held by the river. "They died together," someone said, "let us send them off together."

On the day of the funeral, the university closed its doors so that students could attend. Speeding trucks which usually carried vetiver roots to a nearby perfumery drove slower than usual. Street vendors abandoned their wares to attend the funeral. Laborers, who ritualistically paced for miles in search of work they seldom found, were noticeably absent from the roads. The school bus, still partly submerged in the river, formed the backdrop for the service. Nineteen caskets were lined in perfect formation along the riverbank.

"Gran Mèt la bay; God giveth. Gran Mèt la pran; God taketh away . . ." The usual platitudes would not console the crowd.

The pastor commended Jean-Max and his schoolmates for their effort. He applauded Boursicault's magnanimous gesture, saying: "That man is worth his weight in the gold Haitians need in order to buy back our dignity, amen?"

"Amen," the crowd affirmed.

Jean-Max nodded. Monsieur Boursicault's gift spared the families the added grief of having to go deep into debt to send their children off appropriately.

"They were our little sisters, brothers, our nieces and nephews." The pastor waved one of the memorial pamphlets which Monsieur Boursicault had distributed to the attendees. "They were our grandchildren, our godchildren; they were our sun in the day and our stars in the night sky, amen?" He read the victims' names, pausing after each one, allowing family members equal time to weep.

"They were our children," the pastor continued. "But they did not belong to us. They were not our possessions. Their real Father has called them home. We must thank Him for each day He allowed those children to be in our midst. Amen?"

The multitude responded with a reluctant "Amen."

When the pastor read the names of Madan Louisaint's girls, she posed the only question to which she hoped he had an answer: "Why?"

"God's will is not our own," the pastor replied.

"Why?" Madan Louisaint screamed again. The crowd held its breath, waiting anxiously for the pastor to provide a suitable answer.

"Let us remember that God, too, lost a Son. His only begotten Son."

"He took my babies," Madan Louisaint wailed.

Jean-Max, who had accompanied Madan Louisaint and her daughter Beatrice to the funeral, patted the woman gently on the back.

She was grateful for Jean-Max's presence. Had her husband not disappeared across the Dominican border a few years earlier, he would have been the one standing beside her now, propping her up with that soft look that was always in his eyes. How those eyes had pondered the crimson horizon that promised him a better life! He was never seen or heard of again. "Ti moun mwen yo ale," Madan Louisaint mumbled to Jean-Max. "My babies are gone."

Beatrice's eyes brimmed with tears too. She cried for her mother, her sisters, and herself. The familiar stomach pain that had kept her from boarding the ill-fated bus was now twisting her insides so much that she found it difficult to breathe. She said nothing of the needles stinging her insides. She understood that no one—not even her mother—could help her now. The others, the ones in the caskets, were more important.

"Take heart," Jean-Max whispered to Madan Louisaint.

Madan Louisaint screamed another blistering "Why?"

The pastor struggled on: "God's ways are not our ways." There was not a hint of doubt in his voice. "The children may be gone from us, but God has not left us. He will never leave or forsake us."

"Why?" Madan Louisaint was so overcome with zezisman that she collapsed in Jean-Max's arms. A group of mourners swarmed her. They fanned her face with hats, their bare hands, and memorial pamphlets.

"Open your eyes," they urged her.

Beatrice slipped out of the crowd and wandered off in perfect solitude. She found a smooth rock by the river and sat on it.

Everyone was so busy tending to Madan Louisaint and others whose knees, hearts, or minds had given out that they did not see the little girl sitting by herself, studying the pamphlet in her small hands.

Beatrice ran her fingers over her sisters' names, erasing and caressing them simultaneously. She continued to run her fingers over the letters until the thought occurred to her to fold the pamphlet in such a way that it became a little hat. She folded the little hat and now it looked like a funnel. She continued to fold methodically until she had constructed a perfect little boat that she set adrift on the river.

As the mourners clumped around one another several yards away, Beatrice watched the current pull her little boat toward the bus. The water brought a warm tingle to her toes when she stepped into the river to retrieve it. She walked farther, her eyes fixed on the little boat drifting toward the crumpled bus. When the bottom of the river dropped from underneath Beatrice's new shoes and the current caused her freshly pressed hair to crinkle up, her new funeral dress rose above her head, floating on the water like a cluster of lilies.

HERITAGE

Raymond's attempt to scream for help failed. The sound that passed through his throat was so faint that no one heard it. He pressed a hand against his chest, hoping to contain the crushing pain. He lifted his eyes toward the sky, smiling like one who expects some grand thing to happen. Perhaps angels would swoop down through the patches of cloud and whisk him out of the cornfield. Perhaps the ancestors would stand in a receiving line with arms open. He continued to search the sky for angels and ancestors, but all he got in return was the blinding blue space. The noonday sun raged on in its usual merciless way, pounding hot rays into his head.

A feeble breeze swept over the cornstalks and leveled Raymond. He hit the ground with a dull thud. His head scattered the clan of ants that were busy transporting the day's meal to headquarters. Raymond struggled to push himself to his feet, but his arms and legs would not comply. A shaft of light reached him on the ground, revealing a spiraling wall of dust motes through which he beheld the face he hoped still belonged to his wife. *Chérie*, he wanted to say, but his tongue was too heavy.

"Raymond!" The woman's double-edged scream sliced the air as well as the delicate thread still connecting her husband to consciousness. Now there was only darkness, oblivion so bitter that Raymond's mouth frothed.

When consciousness finally returned, he found himself stretched out on the pallet inside the mud hut he shared with his wife and their two children: Frisner and Jean-Max.

Madan Casseus sat on the dirt floor beside her husband, keeping a remarkably steady hand on the cool compress she had placed on his forehead. She sent Frisner to fetch Doktè Massenat. She hoped her son would find the doctor and bring him to the hut before it was too late. (A telephone call would have saved Frisner the hours it took to locate Doktè Massenat, but the Casseus family did not have a telephone—few families in Puits Blain did.) The other boy, Jean-Max, crouched in a corner of the hut, watching.

Frisner said what he always did when he had to get somewhere in a hurry: "Pye sa'm manje m'pa ba-w?" His feet kicked up dust as he ran. His first stop was Madan Louisaint's house, their neighbor.

"Sa k genyen?" she asked as soon as she saw him. "What happened?"

"My father," Frisner heaved. "Papa is ill. I need to find Doktè Massenat."

Madan Louisaint said she did not know where the doctor was. Frisner nodded politely and ran back toward the unpaved road. After running from house to house, Frisner finally found Massenat.

When Frisner brought the doctor to the hut, Madan Casseus explained what had happened to the best of her knowledge: "Mari'm endispoze. Li tonbe tankou yon sak diri. My husband collapsed like an empty bag of rice."

The doctor removed his hat and fanned his face. The heat inside the hut was indescribable. (Perhaps the grave would be as hot, the doctor pondered secretly; perhaps Hell—though he did not believe in the existence of the latter.)

"Yes, I see," Doktè Massenat said to Madan Casseus as he removed the handkerchief from his breast pocket. He shook the thing open and carpeted a little spot on the dirt floor next to the patient.

The examination lasted for as much time as it would have taken Madan Casseus to fry an egg on a sizzling three-rock fire. The doctor pressed a couple of fingers against Raymond's neck and nodded in response to whatever cryptic code it communicated.

Madan Casseus twisted the hem of her housedress nervously. "What's wrong with my husband?"

"Shhh." The doctor peeled back Raymond's eyelids and inspected what was underneath with as much consideration as a mechanic at a junkyard peering under the hood of a totaled car for parts. He then turned toward Madan Casseus while shaking his head in an *oh well* manner. "Your husband should be in the hospital," he said as he rose to his feet. The jar of camphor in his bag would be useless in this case.

"Kisa mari-m genyen?" Madan Casseus's voice cracked. "What's wrong with my husband?"

The doctor had seen Raymond's condition before in patients who almost always ended up in one of Boursicault's chain of funeral parlors. He hunched his shoulders, saying, "Your husband is not doing well, but the doctors in Port-au-Prince are very skilled. They'll be able to help him." It was a lie, but the complex message which Raymond's eyes had conveyed told Massenat that a miracle, not medicine, was in order. And since he did not believe in miracles, he offered her the lie which he reserved for just such occasions.

Doktè Massenat picked up his handkerchief. He shook the dust on Raymond absentmindedly. "The doctors in Port-au-Prince have the experience, the equipment, and the medicine to treat your husband." He cleared the lies out his throat.

Madan Casseus eyed Massenat's medicine bag disdainfully. Moments before she had looked at it with hope, believing it contained something that could heal her husband. She was nodding in agreement now. The doctor was right, his raggedy bag couldn't possibly contain anything sophisticated enough to help her husband. She would take Raymond to the hospital at once.

Doktè Massenat had an uncanny ability to foresee situations that would inconvenience him. This special skill enabled him to anticipate Madan Casseus's next question. And before she could ask it, he said: "I wish I could drive you to the hospital myself, but I have another emergency across town." It's not really a lie, Doktè Massenat thought. Someone always needed him. Doktè Massenat took his leave, also taking the sliver of hope his presence had brought.

Madan Casseus reached into her bra and removed a few crumpled gourdes. She gave the money to Frisner. "Go to Kalfou Djoumbala and bring a taptap back here. Quick."

Frisner ran as fast as he could, mumbling, "Pye, sa'm manje m'pa ba-w? Feet, when have I ever eaten and not fed you?" He repeated the words over and over until he reached the corner of Kalfou Djoumbala, where tap-tap drivers waited in endless lines for passengers who hadn't heard about the futility of traveling to Port-au-Prince to look for employment. Frisner hired the first available driver and rode back to his parents' hut.

The taptap driver helped hoist Raymond's body onto the enclosed flatbed. Madan Casseus and her boy children rode in silence. Each time the taptap swerved to avoid pedestrians, Raymond rolled like a bag of merchandise. When they eventually reached the hospital, the driver helped carry Raymond through a long corridor, where women in their final moments of pregnancy and various stages of undress waited with thighs wide open and stunned looks in their eyes.

One of the travailing women took a look at Raymond and said: "The morgue is on the other side."

Madan Casseus ignored the woman, making her way toward the large waiting room filled with people suffering from gunshot wounds, machete gashes, and an assortment of other afflictions. The receptionist instructed her to take a seat—if she could find one—and wait. Madan Casseus and her boys crouched in a corner of the large room; Raymond was stretched out on the floor by their feet.

A lifetime later, when Madan Casseus's name was called and a doctor in bloodstained scrubs examined Raymond, she was told that her husband had suffered a stroke.

"You can leave him here," the doctor suggested in the monotone of an overworked embalmer. "It's up to you," he added, as if she had asked permission to tie a goat to his fence post. "I don't know if we can fix him," he said with passionless objectivity—as if Raymond were a taptap's tire that had gone flat. "But we can keep him for you and watch him for a while. If you can pay."

"I can pay." Madan Casseus sucked her teeth. "Please, just help my Raymond."

With Raymond suddenly stricken, Madan Casseus became her household's sole provider. The money she made by selling fried food to taptap drivers and their passengers at Kalfou Djoumbala would not be enough to feed the boys and cover hospital bills as well. So, without hesitation, Madan Casseus did the one thing she never thought she would. She took the deed to the acres of land her father had bequeathed her and began to parcel out her inheritance.

As news of her circumstances spread, speculators scurried from all corners of the island to secure a piece of Puits Blain. The land which Madan Casseus owned was lush. Paradisiacal. The acres were covered with avocado, lemon, mango, sweetsop, royal palm, and coconut trees. There were breadfruit and almond trees of which everyone in the village heartily partook. Madan Casseus was a wealthy landowner. But because it never occurred to her to sell the land, its monetary value was never counted among her assets.

The offers she received were a pittance of the land's value, but the exigencies of her situation left little time for haggling. Madan Casseus accepted every insulting offer as quickly as it was put upon the little table she had set up under the loofah tree.

The cornfield where Raymond had collapsed was first to go. Boursicault, a sharp entrepreneur from Léogâne, snatched that deal fast. He saw, right away, what others had missed and what Madan Casseus herself had long forgotten. The land which Raymond worked for a few ears of corn sat on a hill that offered a spectacular view of the Caribbean Sea. Boursicault, who was well-known throughout the provinces for his ability to transform any speck of dust into gold, was not interested in raising corn or any other crop on that land. The plans which he had for his life did not include tilling under the scorching sun until sweat leaked out of every pore. He purchased Madan Casseus's cornfield with the sole intention of erasing all evidence that any crop had ever grown there, and building a house larger than the one his imagination had shown him since he was a boy pacing the streets in search of his next meal. The architectural design of Boursicault's house had been etched in his mind for decades: There were pillars and terraces tiled with marble. The house would have a thousand bathrooms (he often quipped), one for every time he had to squat down in the bushes and wipe himself with leaves or pieces of old newspaper. There would be a large kitchen with every modern convenience known to man. The largest and most expensive refrigerator would be filled with champagne—a bottle for every birthday he had wanted to celebrate but could not because there had never been enough money, a bottle for every so-called friend who could not be found when the time came to sing "*Bonne anniversaire, nos voeux les plus sincères.*" And there would be a bottle for every piece of charcoal he had to sell over the years before fate directed him to go into the most profitable business there was: the funeral business. But most importantly, Boursicault determined, every room of his house would boast a huge window from which to view his very own piece of the Caribbean Sea.

Within days of his purchase, Boursicault enclosed the cornfield with a fence so high that even birds had trouble and kept flying into it. He brought in bulldozers and other machines that razed Raymond's hard work, annihilating his perfectly good crop.

Everyone in Puits Blain was so fascinated by their new neighbor that they could not stop talking about him. They asked themselves how it was that Boursicault could walk among them—on the same dirt roads—and never get dust on his shoes. How did he manage to keep his shirts so fresh-looking when everyone else's had sweat stains under the arms and around the collars? Never before had someone of his caliber made Puits Blain his home. What did he really want with the area? With the people who lived there? Men with Boursicault's money usually flocked to exclusive communities in the hills above Pétionville. Men like that lived among their own kind.

The suspicious stares and general distrust came to a halt when one of the villagers suggested that Boursicault's decision to build his residence in Puits Blain was simply a sign that times were changing, that the area was now as desirable a place to live as the hills above Pétionville.

Madan Casseus did not have time to care about who Boursicault was and how he chose to spend his time. He paid cash for the cornfield; that was all that mattered. It did not interest her that the man to whom she had sold her land had started out selling ten cent scoops of charcoal to passersby at the marketplace when he was barely six years old. By his tenth birthday, Boursicault had a clientele so loyal that all other vendors were forsaken in favor of the charming boy who gave his customers a little bit extra—always a little more than they paid for. Boursicault became known for his charm as well as his bold generosity. In a country where gift-giving was rare, Boursicault made it his trademark.

Within days, Madan Casseus's inheritance was mostly gone. She kept only two acres: one for each of her boys. Frisner and Jean-Max would never have to beg anyone for a place to lay their heads at night.

She stopped selling fritay to taptap drivers and their famished passengers, and rode to Port-au-Prince every morning to spend the day with Raymond. His condition remained unchanged. He had to be spoon-fed the drops of bread soup that was his only sustenance. One side of his body was still paralyzed, and she had to pay the hospital the equivalent of an acre of land for each day Raymond was in their care.

During the few visits when Raymond was coherent, he demanded to be taken home. "Non, chéri," Madan Casseus would say as she fed him drops of bread soup. "The doctors can do more for you than I can at home." Weeks later, when Madan Casseus's money was just about gone, she had no choice but to grant her husband's wish.

As soon as they reached the hut, Madan Casseus sent Frisner to fetch Boss Pyè, a leaves doctor about whom she'd heard it said that even though he could not read or write, when his lwa spirits mounted him, that man could speak seven languages.

Boss Pyè was in his fifties. He had bony cheeks, leathery skin, a drunkard's eyes, and a broad smile of saffron-colored teeth. His large fingers were heaped with homemade rings that were topped with chunks of raw amber. He was soft-spoken but so confident that words fell from his lips with the echo of absolute truth. The karabela pants and matching shirt swung from his skeletal frame as if from a wire hanger. The woven djak-out bag slung over his shoulder contained candles, desiccated chicken feet, a flask of sugarcane moonshine, a whistle, and a rainbow of satin handkerchiefs.

Boss Pyè bent over Raymond's crumpled frame and looked carefully into the patient's dim eyes. Then he rubbed his hands together as he sang an invocation to summon the spirits that would assist him. He made circular movements with his hands over the length of Raymond's body, not touching it, lest the illness was contagious. The leaves doctor's diagnosis came after just a few seconds: "Li pran yon koush poud. Someone threw powder on your husband."

Madan Casseus clutched her shirt collar and gasped. It had not occurred to her that something other than natural causes was responsible for her husband's condition.

"But don't worry," Boss Pyè added with a flick of his hand. "I will root out the evil your enemy has planted in your husband's body."

Madan Casseus sighed.

"How long has he been like this?" asked Boss Pyè.

"Many weeks."

"Why you didn't send for me sooner?"

"I put him in the hospital in Port-au-Prince," Madan Casseus said regretfully, "but the doctors there could not help him."

"You wasted a lot of time." The leaves doctor opened his djakout and removed the chicken feet. He ran the dried claws along the length of Raymond's bad arm, leg, and the twisted mouth while chanting in a scratchy baritone. "The person who did this to your husband knows you very well," Boss Pyè clenched his fists. "Could be a neighbor. A relative. Someone who's been in your house. Eaten from your plates. This person is jealous of you."

"Jealous?" Madan Casseus sucked her teeth. "What do I have that anyone would want?" She searched her mind for a face that might belong to her enemy; none appeared.

She and Raymond did not have many friends, but they had no enemies either. When company came, which was seldom, they were received under the loofah tree. As for family members, most of Madan Casseus's kinfolk, la fanmi Desormeau, left Puits Blain years ago. They never visited. They liquidated every piece of land they had inherited and used the cash to get as far away as they could.

"I can't think of anyone who would be jealous of me," Madan Casseus went on.

"You own good land," Boss Pyè replied. "Your ancestors left you a nice heritage."

"I sold most of it to pay the hospital."

"Yes, I know. But there is more."

"Two acres," Madan Casseus said. "One for each of my boys."

Boss Pyè gave her hand a reassuring squeeze. "Normally, I charge two thousand dollars US to drive out the kind of evil spirit that's on your husband. Because your situation is so bad, I will do the work for one thousand. But when I'm through"—his voice was like thunder—"when I'm through, your husband will be better than new. And your enemy won't be able to touch him ever again."

Madan Casseus did not have one thousand dollars left. As if he could read her mind, Boss Pyè said: "Give me five hundred American dollars now. We'll work something out for the rest. Your husband's health is more important than money, yes?"

He studied the subtle changes in his client's face. Sensing her reluctance, he added: "There is no time to waste, Madan Casseus. We must begin treatment today. Your enemy's magic is powerful, but I can make a more powerful magic to counter it. All you have to do is decide. Now."

Madan Casseus reached into her bra and pulled out a clump of damp bills. She counted five hundred dollars and gave them to Boss Pyè. He stuffed the cash into his pocket before reaching into his djakout for several candles.

"Make your demands to the spirit world," Boss Pyè instructed. "Your husband will be like new before the last of these seven candles burns out."

Madan Casseus nodded.

"You'll need a young unspotted goat," Boss Pyè continued. "Usually, I purchase all the provisions myself, but since I'm giving you such a discount already, you'll have to buy the goat yourself."

Madan Casseus nodded again.

"Slaughter the goat and mark your doorpost with the blood to keep your enemy from crossing your threshold. Take a plate of the cooked meat to a crossroads and make your demands there too. Put the plate down. Then walk away without turning around to see what may be behind you. If you hear someone whisper, don't answer. Whatever you do, don't turn around. Wrap the goat's head, one hind and one front leg in a strong burlap bag. Take the bundle to the cornfield where your enemy tried to steal your husband's soul. Declare that you want Raymond back whole, and then put the bundle in the ground. Do as I say, Madan Casseus. I promise you your Raymond will be better than new."

Madan Casseus's lips quivered. She had heard of people taking part in such rituals, but never imagined that she would be counted among them.

"As you do these things," Boss Pyè concluded, "I will be working on your behalf from my own home. I will leave no stone unturned in the spirit world. Do you understand?"

Madan Casseus nodded.

"I will not stop calling on the spirits until your husband is well again. Do you understand me?"

"Yes," Madan Casseus mumbled. "Thank you very much, Boss Pyè."

The leaves doctor flashed a reassuring smile as he walked out of the hut.

An unspotted goat was purchased, slaughtered, and cooked within hours. The doorpost was marked, as the leaves doctor had prescribed. Madan Casseus fixed a plate to take to the crossroads. She carried the goat's head and legs in a burlap bag. She would bury the bundle in the cornfield.

Darkness cloaked the unpaved roads leading to the crossroads. Madan Casseus was not alone in the street. She did not see anyone, but she knew many eyes were watching her.

When she reached the corner and placed the plate of food down, she heard what sounded like the gallop of horses. She did not turn around—just as Boss Pyè had advised. She closed her eyes and issued her demand to the spirit world: "Make my Raymond well again."

The gallop drew nearer. There was now a gathering of shadows a few feet away from the spot where Madan Casseus was crouched. But she dared not look. She kept her eyes fixed on the task before her and her thoughts on Raymond. Something or someone was now standing inches behind her, taking breaths like a man, heaving as if it had run a great distance.

Madan Casseus never turned around to see what was behind her. She stood up and began walking in the direction of the cornfield, determined to carry out her assignment.

"Whatever you are," Madan Casseus said to the shadows behind her, "take the food and leave my husband alone."

Had she disobeyed Boss Pyè's orders and turned around, she would have seen a group of street children waiting impatiently for her to leave so that they could divide the food among themselves. Those children were always thankful for people like Madan Casseus who brought food for spirits that they never once saw.

When Madan Casseus reached the cornfield, she

dug a little grave with the large wooden spoon she had brought specifically for what was considered the most important part of her mission. "Take this goat's head and give me back my husband the way you found him," she said.

The shadows and sounds at the crossroads anchored in Madan Casseus's mind Boss Pyè's story that spirits roamed the unpaved roads, waiting for unsuspecting men and women engaged in the most wholesome midnight errands.

"What are you doing here?" The disembodied voice startled Madan Casseus. She tried to hide but the new proprietor recognized her right away. He had gotten such a good deal on the land that he could not forget the woman who gave it to him.

Madan Casseus was now shaking with a combination of fear and regret. Boursicault had taken her by surprise. She did not expect him to be in the field at such a late hour. She'd heard it said that Boursicault was a peculiar man who liked to walk in the old field day and night—to clear his head. Raymond had spent his life sweating in that field and now Boursicault was using it to *clear* his head?

Monsieur Boursicault leaned on the carved mahogany walking stick which he carried strictly as an accessory, and repeated his question a little more forcefully: "What in the hell are you doing on my property?"

He hated to shout at her. He hated to have to kick her off his property, but she was doing the one thing in the world he detested. Boursicault almost apologized, but stopped himself just in time.

Madan Casseus could have been his mother. His

own mother had taken part in those archaic rituals. It was during one of those ceremonies that he ran away from home long ago, vowing never to return. He had become a street child, like one of those kids who had stood behind Madan Casseus when she placed that plate of food down at the crossroads. How he used to thank the stars for women like her who brought heaps of food, juice, and candy galore for the spirits.

Boursicault recalled the sweet Novembers of his youth. He could live for weeks on the food left for spirits which he—in all his years on the street—never once ran into. But he did run into thousands of other motherless children who called the streets home and women like Madan Casseus who never had the courage to look behind them.

"Just passing through," Madan Casseus replied in a small voice. She regretted selling the cornfield to such an inconsiderate man. But what else was she to have done? She needed money to try and save her husband.

Boursicault moved in closer. He looked disapprovingly at the little grave she had dug and the bundle she was preparing to bury in it. "I don't want people to pass through. That's why I have the fence."

"The gate was open!" Madan Casseus cried out. "Time is running out for my husband."

Boursicault prodded the bundle with his walking stick. "What's in it?" he asked, in spite of himself.

He could not care less if the bag contained food, money, or charcoal. It was the absurdity of the act that annoyed him. He knew about her husband's sickness. He'd heard that the man had suffered a stroke in the cornfield. How would burying some bizarre bundle in the field help him?

"A little goat's head." Madan Casseus had not meant to tell the truth; the words glided out of her mouth involuntarily. Boursicault had that effect on people. There was never a need to make up stories for men like him. *Those who deal in death hear it all. The road to the grave is paved with stories.* What unfathomable thing had he not heard?

"Get off my land!" Boursicault shouted, secretly wanting to help Madan Casseus to her unsteady feet, as he would have done for his own mother. He wanted to assure her that nothing would have resulted from her mission. Burying a goat's head on his property would not have changed her husband's condition. He resisted the urge to comfort her.

Madan Casseus opened her arms. "Please, Misye Boursicault. Someone threw powder on my husband. The doctors at the hospital couldn't help him. If I don't bury this here, my Raymond will die. Please, Misye Boursicault. They say you're a good man. Please . . ."

"Get off my land and take your garbage with you!" Boursicault blasted. "And if I catch you here again, thunder strike me down, I'll break your skull open with this cane." He walked away and disappeared in the darkness.

Defeated, Madan Casseus scooped up the bundle and staggered back to her hut with the coordination of a child who couldn't stop tasting the bottle of kleren moonshine he was sent to buy. She would have to wait until morning to send Frisner for Boss Pyè. Perhaps he would prescribe an alternative to her failed attempt in Boursicault's field.

"Hurry," Madan Casseus said to her son as soon as morning came.

"*Pye, sa'm manje m'pa ba-w?*" Frisner recited his mantra as he ran. When he reached Boss Pyè's compound, he found him sitting at a card table with a group of men, each with a shot glass before him. The festivities from the previous night had spilled into the morning without them realizing it.

"Manman needs to see you," Frisner announced.

Boss Pyè muttered something under his breath and sent the contents of his shot glass down his throat with a violent motion. He placed his cards facedown on the table before leaving with the messenger. The others also drank from their shot glasses and placed their own cards facedown on the table. The game would resume as soon as Boss Pyè returned.

"Those hypocrites enrage me," Boss Pyè scowled once Madan Casseus explained what had taken place on Boursicault's property. "They know more about this stuff than I do, but they pretend not to. I suppose it's just not civilized, not moun-de-byen enough for them."

"What do I do now?" Madan Casseus sighed.

"There is another way," Boss Pyè declared. "But that will cost a little more."

"I have no money left."

"You don't need cash. I'll take a couple of acres off your hands and call it even."

"I have two sons. If I give you the little land I have left, what will they have to call their own when I am gone?"

"It's your decision," said the leaves doctor. "You can have your husband back on his feet, or you can keep the land for your sons. But believe me: I can see by the way Frisner runs that he will get as far away from Puits Blain as soon as he can. And as for Jean-Max, he will follow his brother's lead and leave this place too. This country is going down, Madan Casseus, don't you see? Your land won't be worth five pennies in five years. You have a chance to use it now for something good. You must. Yes?"

"I'll take my chances," Madan Casseus replied. "I'll rest better in my grave knowing that my children have a piece of land to call their own."

"What about your husband?" Boss Pyè rubbed his chin. "He's going to die if you don't finish the work we've started."

"He might."

"Suit yourself, Madan Casseus. Just don't call me when Raymond starts plowing cornfields on the other side of life. I don't know anything about raising the dead."

"I can see that," Madan Casseus said. "I can see that now."

RAYMOND CASSEUS

Nine months after suffering the massive stroke that would have killed most men, Raymond Casseus was still waiting for angels to swoop down and birth him out of the newly disfigured body now riddled with bedsores. Bitterness filled him when he realized that quite possibly he would not die, and that the farthest away he would get from the pallet inside the hut was not some paradisiacal garden on the other side of the sky but the shady spot under the loofah tree where he used to sit, long ago, on sunny Sunday afternoons listening to Alsibyad tell jokes on the radio. The one about the poor bridegroom in need of a wedding suit was Raymond's favorite. He retold that story countless times to anyone who would listen:

"Mon konpè, I am deeply honored that you would ask me to be your best man. That's the only reason why I'm even considering lending you my good suit to get married in. If I do lend you the suit, however, you must promise that you will not sit down during the ceremony or at the reception afterward, lest you wrinkle it up too much.

"If the priest asks you to kneel, don't. Pretend you're deaf! The priest won't bother you if he thinks you're deaf. Just stand there and keep standing until the part where *he tells you to kiss the bride, et cetera, et cetera. Stand as straight you can too, because I hate those creases that crooked men get around the shoulders and back.*

"And whatever you do, mon konpè, try not to put your hands in the pockets either. My hands, as you can see, are not rough like a travayè. They're silky like a president's. See, no calluses. I wouldn't want you to snag the fabric or burst a seam and make the pocket openings too wide. Understand?

"Also, please be sure that you do not eat cake during the reception. I don't want crumbs in the breast pocket. Don't drink anything either, unless it's clear like water. It costs too much to get stains out these days. The suit's made of the most delicate polyester. Someone sent it to me from New York.

"And, mon konpè, be sure not to dance too close to the bride. You might get excited and sweat around the armpits and God knows where else.

"The more I think about it, mon konpè, the more inclined I am not to lend you my good suit. You're like a brother to me. I would hate to have something so trivial ruin our relationship."

In all those months Raymond did not utter a single word; not even a sigh passed through his lips. What was there to say anyhow? Life as he had known it had shattered. No amount of talking would reverse the situation and bring the pieces back together again. The decision to shut down half of his body was made for him. The decision to shut his mouth up for good was one that *he* made deliberately. He used only his eyes to communicate: *Raymond, are you hungry? Blink once. Raymond, are you in pain? Blink twice. Raymond, are you tired? Stare into the distance. Raymond, would you like to go outside and sit under the loofah tree for a little while? Squeeze the eyes shut.*

During this reversed gestation period, Madan Casseus gave up hope that her husband would return to his old self. Life with Raymond had been peaceful and sweeter than cinnamon scones in condensed milk. Their daily routine of backbreaking labor was a fate they had accepted with grace. They would toil, side by side, until death wrenched them apart. They would work for as long as they had breath in their bodies—for their children, Frisner and Jean-Max.

Raymond and his wife had dreamed for their boys a different life than the one they lived: Frisner and Jean-Max would study at the university and become bona fide philosophers. They would spend their days studying, not standing under the unforgiving sun, tilling land or selling fried food on the street. Her boys would be educated. Their world would be one of books, suits, and neckties. They would ride in cars, not on mules. Their shoes would be polished, not layered with dust that let everyone know they were hut-dwelling peasants. They would not be X-signers like their parents.

Raymond and his wife had not feared death. The end, they knew, was as natural a part of life as the sun leaking through the thatched roof during the day and the moon at night. But the idea of being stretched out on the pallet with a constellation of blisters on Raymond's skin was not something they had pictured. It never occurred to Madan Casseus that Raymond might lose the part of his brain that made it possible for him to speak or hold a spoon up to his mouth. Or hold her in his arms and retell those Alsibyad jokes he liked so much. He had always been so strong. So indestructible.

Madan Casseus panicked when she found Raymond half-dead in the cornfield, his head on a trail of ants that bit him without him even noticing. The ants on Raymond's face had troubled her. Fear had shaken every speck of reason out of her head. She scolded herself now for the acres of land she had liquidated; the fortune she gave away to the leaves doctor and the hospital.

And now, as she sat holding the cold compress on Raymond's forehead, she noticed that the twist of his lips had relaxed a little. He had also moved a few inches from where she had placed him last. She had stopped hoping for miracles long ago, but wasn't he looking at her differently now?

"Chérie," Raymond croaked, "help me to my feet. I want to sit under the loofah tree. If it's still there."

Madan Casseus did not blink. "Of course the loofah tree is still there." She spoke in such a casual manner, but inside she was leaping with pleasure. Her Raymond could talk again. Her Raymond would be whole again.

Raymond had forgotten everything that had happened to him in the nine months since he collapsed in the field and his head hit that trail of ants that disturbed his wife so. He could still see her sunlit face inches from his. He could hear her calling his name and screaming for help. Everything else was murky: he did not recall the weeks at the hospital, the leaves doctor. And thank God he missed the part where Madan Casseus parted with her fortune in land.

What he did remember was the life he had before he collapsed; the food he loved, the music he liked. He remembered sitting under the loofah tree on Sundays, eating corn and listening to Alsibyad.

For nine months he lived on nothing but bread soup for breakfast, boiled breadfruit for lunch, and plantain mush for supper—baby food that did not need to be chewed; bare sustenance intended solely to keep him from starving to death. Absent from his plate were the flavors that used to make him take Madan Casseus by the waist, spin her around, and dip her while she shouted at him to let her be.

Raymond Casseus loved his rice white with a mountain of conch meat. And if Madan Casseus had time to slice an avocado and sprinkle a few pieces of pikliz on top, there was no telling what he would do to express his gratitude. "Can you make me a little conch and some rice?" he was now saying to a stunned Madan Casseus who continued to hold the compress over his head, not moving lest he stop talking and fall back into that world where nothing moved. "Sprinkle some pikliz on top for me."

"Yes," Madan Casseus replied. Everything Raymond said was met with the same "Oui, chéri mwen" response, though she didn't budge. The truth was, Madan Casseus was not sure whether or not she was dreaming or wishing so desperately that Raymond would speak to her that she had convinced herself that sounds were coming out of his mouth.

She sat there in a state of disbelief until Frisner came into the hut and heard his father. The boy jumped up so high his head hit the thatched roof.

Madan Casseus said: "Calm yourself down, boy, and help me get your father to the loofah tree so that I can make him a little conch and some rice."

MADAN CASSEUS

Madan Casseus bunched her skirt between her thighs and reclined between the exposed roots of the loofah tree.

She sighed, stretched her legs, and rubbed her knees. She contemplated the gray ashes that clogged the furrows crisscrossing the skin beneath which lay barely working joints that creaked like rusty hinges of old doors.

She arched her back against the tree as if the ridges in the bark were fingers that could massage those spots where an assortment of aches had taken residence without the slightest inclination to vacate.

She dropped her head and shoulders forward. The muscles tried to recall the elasticity they once possessed, but could not. She closed her eyes, mumbling absentmindedly to herself.

Her lower back had stored in its memory the strain of every load she'd lifted from the ground to the saddle, and from the saddle to the unpaved street corner where she sold fritay every dawn for ten thousand years.

Customers treasured Madan Casseus's fried yam, plantain, and sausage. The sun showed its indifference by routinely frying her. Her back had also memorized the times her boy children used her body to enter the world. That memory had always been sweet. Until now.

A few pipirit, hidden in the loofah tree's branches, serenaded her. Madan Casseus was thankful for their soothing song. The birds were grateful too. They knew better than anyone that a few swift blows of a sharp ax would turn their refuge into firewood and their easy, *isn't-life-wonderful?* melody into a dirge.

Madan Casseus puffed on her wooden pipe mechanically as Frisner approached. "Manman," his deep voice silenced the pipirit. The loofah's branches shaded his face from the spiteful sun. An occasional breeze rustled the leaves, scattering a few dried ones in the stifling air.

"In this country," Frisner said, "when people see that you're poor, they forgive you because they know it's not your fault. Poverty grows inside a man's house like weeds in a garden. You can pull them out, but they always come back. But when people see you living in a hut, they want to spit in your face because they say there's no excuse for it. Anyone can build a decent house to live in these days. A few sacks of cement, a few blocks, and a little imagination; it doesn't take that much. The mud hut is a symbol of everything that's wrong with Haiti today. You need to tear it down."

Madan Casseus fixed her eyes on her thatched roof hut a few yards away. She kept her mouth shut.

"The old folks are the ones holding us back," Frisner continued. "They're happy to live out their lives in misery. They wrap their heads with rags, raise scrawny chickens and goats, and then puff on their pipes like peasants in the countryside. If Haiti is ever to move forward, the old generation has to accept the fact that times have changed. They have to change too."

Madan Casseus sucked on her pipe. She listened but remained silent.

Frisner wouldn't quit: "Ever since Boursicault built his house down here, many important families have made Puits Blain their home. They see how valuable the area is. They've invested—"

"Stealing isn't investing," Madan Casseus interrupted. "You ought to measure your mouth before you talk. These important families you're talking about didn't do anything but steal land from poor, desperate people."

"However they got here," Frisner's voice rose a little, "they're here. Under our eyes, forcing us to watch them. They make us look bad."

Madan Casseus said: "I make you look bad. Isn't that what you mean to say?"

Frisner pretended not to hear. "The important families have built palaces with swimming pools and tennis courts. They can't possibly enjoy looking at this hut on their way home every day."

"If you don't have the balls to say what you mean," Madan Casseus countered, "why don't you shut your snout?" She sucked her teeth again and spat angrily.

Frisner shifted his body to avoid the spit. "I'm trying to tell you what we mean. Manman, your hut is the last one standing in Puits Blain. It doesn't take much. I can demolish your shack in one day and build you something with a proper nose on its face. You always told me to conduct myself with pride, but this hut is a source of shame. To you."

"I've told you before," Madan Casseus gritted her teeth, "I don't want your new house. I like the one I've got."

Frisner shook his head in exasperation. "Just the other day a mulatto from Kenscoff came around here searching for land. He took one look at your hut and walked away. I guess he didn't want a thatched-roof shack for a view. What civilized person would?" He did not wait for an answer. "Why do you think Boursicault and the others built their fences up so high? They don't want to see this hut and I don't blame them."

"Leave me in peace," Madan Casseus said.

"I am a professional man now. I am a mechanic. My mother should not live like this. I may not be rich, but I can build you a decent place to live. The neighbors would stop wagging their tongues then. Just the other day a man I'd never seen before looked right in my face and said he'll torch your hut if we don't tear it down."

"And what did you tell that man?"

"I told him I would torch it myself, if my mother was not living in it."

"Strike a match around here, boy, and you'll be the one burning down. I am not playing with you. I've already buried one man I loved. I can do it again. Just say when."

"Manman—"

"Don't call me that, ingrate. If all you want to do is torch my house, get off my land before I throw a bucket of water on you. You should have told that man to go ahead and try to burn down my house. You should have told that bastard to come here and speak those words to my face. I'm not afraid of him. And I'm not afraid of you."

"I could have gotten a machete and threatened to cut off his head, but he would have laughed, Manman. That man disrespected me, but he had every right. As long as you refuse to live in something respectable, how am I supposed to hold my head up around here?"

Madan Casseus pulled herself up to her feet with a groan. She raised her head to meet Frisner's spiteful gaze. "One day you will stop bothering me. I tell you I don't want a new house, but you won't listen. You say the neighbors are talking. Well, let them talk. Ki fout mele mwen avè yo? What do I care? When their bellies get full with my business, they'll throw up and leave me alone. I've never knocked on their door for a piece of bread. Never asked them for a place to put my head. Never begged them for a drop of water. This hut and the land it sits on belong to me. I don't owe the neighbors five cents. Let them talk until they can't talk anymore. One day, when they get tired of minding my business, they'll mind their own. I can wait. One thing I've never lacked is patience."

"Ay, Manman." Frisner reached out to touch her arm, but she slapped his hand away and started to walk toward the hut. He followed her. "All I'm saying is that you deserve better."

"I don't hang my hat where my hands cannot reach," Madan Casseus said. "And I don't fart higher than my butthole."

Frisner shook his head. "See, people don't talk like that anymore either. Those sayings went out with thatched-roof huts. No civilized person would even pretend to understand what those sayings mean."

Madan Casseus cocked two fists on her hips. "I guess you're so civilized now that you figure you can just wash your hands in my face. Can't say I'm not happy for you, though. But if I didn't send you to school, how civilized would you be today? How many years did I spend at Kalfou Djoumbala burning my fingers in hot oil to pay for your tuition, buy your books, and make sure your uniforms didn't have holes in them; make sure you didn't stink? And now listen to you. You're ashamed of my house. I pressed my back down on that dirt floor and pushed you out so you could spit in my face today!"

Frisner followed her into the hut. A red-and-white checkered vinyl tablecloth divided the interior into two rooms. The front area contained a doll-sized chair with a fraying seat. Several cardboard boxes were stacked in one corner; an old quilt was thrown over them. There were two aluminum cups and a calabash bowl with a spoon in it on a small table.

On the other side of the checkered tablecloth was Madan Casseus's sleeping area. The pallet was rolled up and leaning in the corner. Several old dresses, which she never wore, hung from a hook in the wall. There was one window with a view of the loofah tree and the outhouse beyond.

As Madan Casseus moved about, dust rose from the dirt floor.

"I've talked to the New York cousins."

"I hope you didn't mention my name to them."

"They've applied for traveling papers. For me. They're trying to get me to come over there. I can get work. Make a good living. Send you money—"

"I don't need your money."

"I had to change my name to Desormeau. I was never really a Casseus. There was a mistake on my birth certificate. Whoever filled out the paperwork never wrote the words *Raymond Casseus* anywhere. I was not given my father's name. No one ever noticed. You never noticed. How would you have known? But I fixed that, Manman. My birth certificate now says *Frisner Desormeau*. I fixed the problem."

"Shut your mouth."

"I'm a Desormeau now, just like the New York cousins. If things work out, I might leave Haiti in a few months. They promise to work hard on getting me out of here as fast as they can."

"Did the New York cousins also promise you a three-legged cow? Be careful, Frisner. Don't fart too high—"

"Please," Frisner sighed.

"I hope you never mentioned my name to those New York cousins. I never wanted those Desormeau people to know anything about me." Her eyes brimmed with tears. "How long have they been gone? How long have we been dead to them? Do they ever write us?"

"They say they sent many letters."

"Did you ever receive one?"

"Manman, you know how the mail system is in this country."

"Fool." Madan Casseus pulled the quilt off the boxes in the corner and opened the top one. She removed an old cookie canister that contained needles and a few spools of thread. She carried the canister and the quilt out of the hut.

Frisner was only inches behind her as she made her way back to the loofah tree. He did not offer to help as his mother struggled to slip thread through a needle. She succeeded after a while, and met her son's bitter gaze with bitterness of her own.

He was like a vulture waiting for a body to die before he picked it apart. Madan Casseus kept her eyes on the tattered quilt in her hands. She inserted the needle in one side of the fabric and pulled it out from the other. The needle trembled between her fingers.

"The dirt floor, the thatch roof, the mosquitoes, the tic blood on the walls, the little window, and even the stifling air inside that hut all belong to me." She spoke as if no one was listening. "Dozens of hurricanes have passed over my house and could not touch it. I've seen winds rip trees right out of the ground, but they were never strong enough to move my house one foot." She gave a small laugh, but there were tears in her eyes. "I gave birth to you in that hut. I nursed and clothed you. After your father died, I made sure you went to school so that no one would count you among the blind. Now, you are so much better that you changed your name. Why didn't you just burn my house down while I was sleeping one night instead?"

"My heart breaks for you, Manman." Frisner words had just enough truth in them to sound sincere, but his mother's pain was not made less. "I've tried to tell you for a long time that your house needs to come down, but you refuse to listen."

"Remember Elizo?" Madan Casseus asked in an uncharacteristically small voice.

Frisner grunted. How many times had she told him that story? He was not interested in hearing it again, but knew nothing could stop her from recounting it.

"On the way home from school," she began, "a little boy saw a pipirit skipping from branch to branch. He aimed his slingshot to take down the bird. The bird saw the boy and sang: *Don't kill me, don't kill me, Elizo*. The boy knew by its pretty voice that the pipirit would taste good. *How do you know my name?* Elizo asked, while steadying his hands, taking aim. *Elizo, if you kill me, one day you'll kill your manman too. Elizo, yes. One day you'll kill your manman too, Elizo!*"

"Manman," Frisner held up his hands to stop his mother from continuing. She began to hum the Elizo song, keeping her eyes on her sewing. Frustrated, Frisner walked away without another word.

When he returned several days later to try and talk his mother into letting him demolish her hut, she acquiesced. Within days, Madan Casseus's home was reduced to a pile of rubble.

Frisner worked from morning to night. He knew he would have to leave the country soon. He had kept his appointment with the consul at the American Embassy in Port-au-Prince. He had cried tears that stung his face on their way down to staining his good shirt. He had told the consul all about his dreams of becoming something more. He had said that the United States of America was the only country that could help him reach that goal.

The consul granted Frisner's request enthusiastically. He'd had such a pleasant day that he approved several applications without meaning to. The consul had gotten up on the right side of the bed that morning; breakfast had been particularly delicious; the birds outside his bedroom window had sung the prettiest melody; the applicants had been unusually civil. No one argued when he denied an application. Mothers did not force him to look at photographs of children or husbands they hadn't seen in years. Children did not cut him open with their eyes when he told them he would not reunite them with their parents.

"Good luck," the consul had said to Frisner in English. *Good luck*. Frisner liked those words, even if he did not know what they meant.

He would leave by the end of the month. But not without building his mother a respectable house. There would be no indoor plumbing or electrical wiring, but at least the hut, like his old name, would be obliterated.

ACKNOWLEDGMENTS

This book would not have been possible without the encouragement of M. Lucienne and Jean C. Ulysse; Judy and Lennie; Felicie Montfleury and Lamercie LaFrance; Madan Deo and Manman Louise; sisters in fact and in deed: Gina A. Ulysse and Irmina "Toutou" Ulysse; Elizabeth LaFrance; Daphne, Nadine, Genevieve, and Colin "Se lòzèy" D.; Rachelle, Regine, and Sandy Coriolan; Marie-Marthe and Cindy Jean-Robert; Betty and Marie-France Pierre; Patricia and Elsie D.; Laurie Sauray, Lany Bersch, Rebecca Asofsky, Dorah Pierre, Ruby Worth, Dr. Raquel Rivera, Nora Dellayah, Freysi Moran, Papa Yiyi, "Manman Yaya"; Nadia, Barbara, and França Simeon; F-8's Laura "Bespectacled" Lee, Mary Shine 1 and 2, Sherry I., Courtney B., Sarah K., Jennifer P., and the incomparable Catharine Peace. This book certainly would not have materialized and emerged into proper light without Akashic Books' publisher, Johnny Temple, and his amazing team. Finally, I thank you, the reader, for spending precious time with the characters in *Drifting*.